Ghostly
LINKS

By

Richard L. Baldwin

Ghostly LINKS

Richard L. Baldwin

ISBN:0-9660685-8-0

Published by Buttonwood Press, LLC
P.O. Box 716
Haslett, Michigan 48840
www.buttonwoodpress.com

Other Books
by Richard L. Baldwin

FICTION
Mysteries (no profanity; suitable for teenagers and adults)

A Lesson Plan for Murder (1998)
ISBN: 0-9660685-0-5; Buttonwood Press

The Principal Cause of Death (1999)
ISBN: 0-9660685-2-1; Buttonwood Press

Administration Can Be Murder (2000)
ISBN: 0-9660685-4-8; Buttonwood Press

Buried Secrets of Bois Blanc: Murder in the Straits of Mackinac (2001)
ISBN: 0-9660685-5-6; Buttonwood Press

The Searing Mysteries: Three in One (2001)
ISBN: 0-9660685-6-4; Buttonwood Press

The Marina Murders (2002)
ISBN: 0-9660685-7-2; Buttonwood Press

Moon Beach Mysteries (2003)
ISBN: 0-9660685-8-0; Buttonwood Press

Spiritual

Unity and the Children (2000)
ISBN: 0-9660685-3-X; Buttonwood Press

NON-FICTION

The Piano Recital (1999)
ISBN: 0-9660685-1-3; Buttonwood Press

A Story to Tell: Special Education in Michigan's Upper Peninsula 1902-1975 (1994)
ISBN: 932212-77-8; Lake Superior Press

Acknowledgments

The creation of any book is the work of many people. I wish to thank my editor Gail Garber, my proofreader, Joyce Wagner, my cover designer and typesetter, Marilyn "Sam" Nesbitt. In addition several people were instrumental in offering assistance while the book was being written. Thank you to Amanda Hoffmeister, Pat DeMaagd, Mike Pritchard, and Tom Taylor.

I thank Bill Mory of the Meridian Sun Golf Club for his assistance.

Finally, I thank my wife, Patty Baldwin, for her love, her support, her belief in me, and suggestions for improving this novel. I am blessed beyond blessed to share my life with the woman I lovingly refer to as "The Greatest!"

Dedication

This book is dedicated to my son, Scott Baldwin. Scott and I have enjoyed many rounds of golf in recent years. Scott has much natural ability and specializes in approaching the pin from off the green. I hope he and his sons enjoy playing the game as much as we have. Scott is the father I wish I could have been.

This book is also dedicated to Mike Pritchard. Mike was a classmate of mine at Alma College from 1959-1962. We played on the Alma College Golf Team for three years and enjoyed numerous practice rounds and matches with opponents from schools in the MIAA Conference and elsewhere. Mike is a very unique scholar with a sense of humor. He is a man I respect and admire.

Prologue

Ghostly Links, a beautiful par-72 golf course in the upper Midwest, has consistently been ranked as one of the top ten golf courses in the United States. In addition to being a challenging course, it has a reputation unequal to any other course on the globe. That reputation has to do with things of the spirit.

Within the first nine holes of Ghostly Links is a triangular plot of undeveloped land. Its boundaries are approximately twenty yards beyond the fairway along the 1st, 8th and 9th holes. If you could look down at the Triangle, as many pilots have, you wouldn't see standing water, but thick forestation, tall grass, and plentiful brush. Most people would have no interest in even attempting to walk into the area.

The course opened to the public on July 4, 1999. Eddie Hazard was one of the first golfers to play the course. He went into the Triangle to find his ball and his wife never heard from him again. The theories of what happened range from Native American spirits upset with the tampering of a sacred burial ground to a very strong tug from quicksand. Some have heard he was spotted in California but most don't believe it. There are many other theories as well and the embellishment of the story is only limited by the imagination.

People play Ghostly Links to satisfy their curiosity. At one time or another, ghosts have been seen throughout the course, unexplainable sounds have been heard, and ball movement has been observed that can't be attributed to the wind, hawks, or ground squirrels. But, Ghostly Links is a terrific course, challenging scratch golfers and treating them to a round of golf they will never forget.

Before the Ghostly Links Country Club existed on Long Lake Road, a state mental hospital stood on the property for many years. A doctor by the name of Samuel Sister worked in the medical building on the grounds. Samuel was thought to be eccentric by those who worked with him. In reality, he was brilliant and a true scientist. In fact, there were very few physicians in the Midwest, let alone the country, who worked as diligently to improve the lives of patients with mental illness. Sam was relatively tall at six feet three inches, and his hair was disheveled, mainly because he never took the time to comb it or to get a haircut. He considered such grooming to be time away from his work and therefore, a waste of time.

Dr. Sister did many experiments at the medical facility on the grounds of the hospital and in the early years of the 20th century before there were stringent guidelines for research. Patients had no rights per se, and permission from anyone to carry out an experiment was unheard of.

It was three o'clock on the morning of September 3, 1925 when Dr. Sister, up and working in his laboratory, saw flashing lights and heard a high frequency sound that almost burst his eardrums. He pulled up the shade and looked out. Outside was a gigantic triangular craft. Lights of all colors were swirling about as the smoke of exhaust fumes escaped from the top of the object.

From an opening in the side of the craft came several creatures that were about seven feet tall. They bore some resemblance to human beings in that they stood upright and had appendages similar to the human legs and arms. One seemed much larger and wore a robe that seemed to glow. Dr. Sister was drawn outside to take a closer look at this huge craft.

He was not scared, just curious. At that hour, no one was outside and there were no curious souls arriving to see what had landed.

As Samuel walked toward the tall beings, he was met by the larger alien who was about eight feet tall. He, or perhaps she, had human appendages but no hair and seemed not to have the sense organs of hearing and sight or smell because the area that we would call a head was round in shape but lacked eyes, nose, mouth and ears. However, from somewhere came perfectly spoken English.

Dr. Sister was invited into the large triangular craft and escorted to a council area. He was not threatened, but realized that he was certainly in a strange environment. The best way Dr. Sister would later explain his experience to a colleague was to say that he went into a trance-like state. He was conscious. He was totally at peace and he felt very safe. He made a point to try and remember the dialogue so he could write it down.

After what seemed to be about a half hour, Sam was escorted out of the craft and walked into the hospital and into his laboratory. He watched as the huge triangular craft silently lifted off of the land. It instantly disappeared into space and the ground looked like a giant iron had just left a burn. In this case, the triangular singe was enormous.

The next morning, a maintenance man walked into the Triangle. This man came into the presence of Dr. Sister who recorded his name and implanted a chip in the man's back. Over the next several decades tens of thousands of people would be affected by the Triangle. Most kept secret what had happened to them fearing hospitalization for being mentally unstable. Or, if they did tell someone, the listener was sworn to secrecy.

As our story begins, August 11, 2005, Cliff Hooker, playing 18 holes of golf with his wife Jane, hit his drive into the Triangle. He decided to stand up to the fear that gripped all golfers. He walked into the Triangle to get his Titleist Two.

Chapter One

Thursday, August 11, 2005
Ghostly Links Country Club

Cliff Hooker watched his drive on the first tee curve to the right. From tee to "The Bermuda Triangle of the Links," the trajectory of the ball resembled the outside of a fresh, ripe banana. The ball was hit well and long, but it had been fed to the Triangle where golf balls were never found. Frustrated, Cliff slammed his driver onto the ground. He had every right to be upset. Last Saturday he had a private lesson with golf professional Larry Ball, one of the finest teachers of the game. He had overcome his tendency to slice or at least he did during his lesson.

Larry was a master at analyzing a golfer's swing. In a matter of minutes, with some fine teaching, a duffer's ball was going straight and long. Such joy would often cause the golfer to become ecstatic and throw money and gifts at Larry's feet as if he was a golf god, and to most of his clients, he was.

"Not bad for not being able to see the ball!" Jane said to her rotund husband. She and Cliff seemed to have a perpetual contest to see who could throw the sharpest, yet loving barb at the other. Cliff and Jane had been happily married for 42 years and for 37 of those years had shared hundreds and hundreds of rounds of golf on courses all over the country.

"I know what I did. I brought my hands through a little early," Cliff replied, wiping sweat from his brow.

"Right! Think what you will, Cliff. It's a miracle you hit it! You're lucky if you can see its shadow on the horizon of your belly!"

"I know I can find that ball," Cliff said.

"Not in there, Cliff. You hit it into the Bermuda Triangle. It's gone. Tee up another and forget it."

"Forget it? Forget a brand new Titleist Two? That ball was a gift to me from Larry for doing so well at my lesson. There's good luck written all over that ball, my dear. I'll find it. See that tall pine there?" Cliff said, pointing toward the feared Triangle. "I spotted it there; it'll be resting on pine needles within a twenty-foot radius of the base of that tall pine."

"People don't look for golf balls in the Triangle, Cliff," Jane insisted. "It's gone. Hit another."

"I'm going in to get it," Cliff responded. "The reason others don't go into this mythical area is that people are too lazy to take a minute to find their ball. That's a good ball and I'm not going to let it go to waste."

"You stubborn Scot. Let it go, you fool!" Jane replied, trying to talk some common sense into her husband.

"Not going to," Cliff said. "This myth is perpetuated by a company that is under contract to bring thousands of balls out of ponds and woods only to resell them to the golf course. On a good day, hundreds of dollars' worth of golf balls get hit into the Triangle and who gets rich? The ball-retrieving company and this country club, that's who. All it takes is a golfer to stand up to this hysteria and walk into the Triangle and get his ball. What did that Englishman say, 'All there is to fear is fear itself,' or something like that."

"Churchill, or was it Roosevelt?" Jane asked.

"Yeah, Churchill I think. Roly-poly guy, smoked a cigar, had a way with words. Wait a minute, on second thought, I guess it was Roosevelt. Anyway, whoever said it was right. All there is to fear is fear itself, and folks just need to say to heck with all this superstition and walk right into this Triangle and get their ball!"

"Have it your way, you cheap hacker!" Jane fired off another jab. The two laughed.

Jane went to the red tee box and hit a nice drive, straight and down the middle.

"Nice shot, my dear," Cliff said with envy, but followed his praise with a zinger of his own, "Not long, but straight."

"You betcha it's straight, Clifford," Jane fired back. "This game was never about distance. It's all about accuracy. Accuracy on the greens and accuracy from tee to green. I'll take a short but straight shot any day over a power-packed long ball, no matter what direction it goes."

Cliff Hooker was 63 years old. He'd taken an early buyout from General Motors about three years ago. He wasn't ready to retire and maybe he should have stayed on, but the handwriting was on the wall. The company felt he'd made his contribution. Now he wanted to fish, hunt, play golf, and deal hands of poker for the rest of his years.

Cliff's traditional huge beer belly was not because of beer. It hung out and over his 40-inch belt because he liked to eat, all the time, everything. His cigar, which he chewed but didn't smoke, was forever hanging out of the left side of his mouth. Jane figured Cliff's cause of death would be a race between oral cancer and a heart attack.

Jane Hooker was an excellent golfer who had played golf ever since she was a little girl in Florida. Her father had taken her to play when she was eight years old. Something happened that first day that made her passionate about golf.

After a lifetime of perfecting her game, Jane was often the winner of the women's championship flight. This happened with such regularity that the club pro all but told the engraver to put 'Jane Hooker' on the plaque before the first round of the annual club championship tourney.

Cliff and Jane were a hoot. They were stylish in their dress, wearing knickers and tam-o'-shanters. Their golf equipment was top-notch, golf bags were leather and their clubs were the finest Larry sold in the pro shop. To look at them was to know that quite a bit of money had gone into their passion.

Cliff did not hit another ball. He fully intended to go into the Triangle and find his Titleist Two. Cliff and Jane took their cart down the middle of the fairway. Cliff was the driver and Jane was the passenger.

"You know, a little walk would do you good once in awhile," Jane said, continuing to taunt her husband.

"Oh, no, spare me the get healthy lecture, will ya, Jane. Just for one 18 hole round, let me ride without a guilt trip. OK? Just once, OK?"

"Well, I'm right," Jane insisted. "The founders of the sport fully intended the players to walk. Walking keeps you slim."

"Right, you mean like John Daly, Craig Stadler, Meg Mellon and Laura Davies. They do pretty well for the extra weight they take along."

"Yeah, but they walk all the time. You get carried around like some pharaoh riding on the shoulders of slaves."

"Oh, Jane, Jane, Jane, have mercy for cryin' out loud. Is it not enough that I just put a brand new Titleist in the Triangle without you robbing me of my concentration? How can I think on my next shot when I'm being asked to seek forgiveness for gluttony?"

"Well, walkin' would do you good once in a while and you might give your sweet lips a break from supporting that awful smelling compressed roll of dead leaves you carry around everyday." Jane knew she had hit below the belt with that one. Larry loved to clinch one half of a good Cuban cigar between his teeth and lips.

"That does it! Out, out, out of the cart, Jane! That's the last straw! Get the club you're going to use and walk. I'm goin' to get my ball. If I don't come back, Jane, it's been fun. It really has. You're a great partner, friend, lover, wife, cook, you name it, but you're on my case all the time and a textbook example of how to nag, but you're good, very good. So, if I don't come out of the Triangle, thanks for the shared life. I mean it, I really do."

"Oh, please, Cliff. Give me a break. Go and take a hike in the quicksand, if that's what you want to do."

Jane walked ahead to her ball which was resting on perfect fairway turf. She had a three wood in her hand and smiled as the cart, leaning to the left and carrying her man, moved toward the Triangle. *For all his faults, he was a good man and was certainly good for a laugh,* Jane thought.

Cliff stopped the cart, looked over at Jane as she swung

with grace and ease. She took an easy swing and placed the ball a hundred and ninety yards closer to the par 5 first hole.

"Accuracy, Clifford, accuracy!" Jane shouted.

Cliff waved at her and chuckled, but he knew she was right. Nice and easy and straight would deliver her to the green in fine shape. He knew he'd find his ball, but wouldn't hit it out of the Triangle. He'd declare an unplayable lie and be hitting three, still a hundred yards behind Jane.

Cliff pulled up to the edge of the Triangle and put the brake on the cart which came to rest on a slight incline. He pulled a 2-iron from his bag so he could move the brush around while looking for the ball. He walked right past the warning sign and into the fabled abyss.

Cliff, with his 2-iron, followed the path of least resistance and moved into the thick mass of brambles and swamp-like land. Cliff's vision of a blanket of pine needles under a tall pine was a fairy tale. He couldn't even see the bottom of the tall pine tree, let alone see his Titleist.

Jane walked over to the cart. She certainly wasn't going to follow etiquette and help Cliff find his ball. She advised him to hit another, but he was intent on finding his small, round, compressed, mass of rubber.

In about three minutes, Cliff appeared holding up a fresh Titleist and grinning from ear to ear. "My dear, I stood up to the Triangle and have come out a brave man and the owner of a once-hit beautiful Titleist. From now on, the myth is a thing of the past. All future golfers can enter without fear. That cigar-chewing Churchill, or maybe it was Roosevelt, was one brilliant leader. Oh, what power we have when we face our fears."

"Give me a break, Cliff Hooker!"

"I assume you want a ride to your ball, my dear?"

"Yes, I do, but first, I'll watch your third shot from a drop here next to the Triangle," Jane replied.

Cliff dropped the ball. Thankfully it landed on a clump of grass and appeared to be sitting well for his next shot. Cliff swung and hit it right on the sweet spot. It took off like a bullet but found a large sand trap about one hundred and thirty yards away from the rather small number one green.

"Anxious to get to the beach, Cliff?" Jane said with a smile.

"Hey, I hit it, didn't I? Good shot too. So, some sand is under it instead of grass. What difference does it really make?" Cliff asked.

"None, I suppose, until you get ready to hit your next shot, then it makes all the difference in the world."

The cantankerous couple drove their cart toward Jane's ball.

"Let me get serious for a minute, Cliff," Jane said. "I really feared for you back there. I guess I thought something might happen to you inside that Triangle."

"Thanks for caring, but hogwash. Sure it's thick stuff, but I've been in worse. The guy after Eddie who hit his ball into the Triangle had a yellow streak down his back. He didn't dare to go in to find his ball and then the rumor started about folks disappearing. It stuck. That's how people come to believe in false stuff. All it takes is a rumor."

"Guess you're right on that one, Cliff."

"Of course I'm right! Usually am, aren't I, dear? Come on, admit it."

"Hey, you get lucky on rare occasions, that's all."

The couple arrived at Jane's ball. Jane chose a 5-iron and hit it perfectly causing it to land ten feet left of the flagstick. She'd have a makeable birdie putt.

Jane got in the cart and the two of them drove to a large sand trap. "Hmmm, not my best shot, hitting out of sand," Cliff said.

"Choke the club a bit, play the ball off your right heel, hit behind the ball and follow through," Jane instructed. "Piece of cake."

"Anybody can quote from a textbook, Jane. Knocking it where you want it to go is quite another thing."

Cliff addressed the ball, took a mighty swing and did in fact get it out of the trap, but he displaced a bucket of sand in doing so.

"Nice out, Clifford," Jane said sincerely. "Tough lie you had there."

Cliff took a minute to rake the trap. His next shot was a decent 8-iron. The ball landed near the cup, but rolled on past leaving Cliff an eight-foot downhill putt. He was on in five and would be putting for a bogey six.

Right after Cliff's shot a cart pulled up with a lone male driver. "How you guys doing?"

"Good. You?" Cliff asked.

"Not bad for an old duffer. Say, I saw you go into the Triangle and come out. Am I right?"

"Yup, I broke the spell. Nothing to it. I mean, it is tough territory, but all that business about its being like the Bermuda Triangle is bunk."

"Yeah, but several years ago, some guy went in there and didn't come out."

"His name was Ed Hazard," Cliff said. "Listen, did you know Ed?"

"No, can't say that I did."

"Ed Hazard was a nut. Nice nut, mind you, but a real nut just the same. I'll tell you what really happened. I think he couldn't stand his wife. Ed walked into the Triangle and walked out the other side and kept right on going to California. His wife to this day thinks he got gobbled up by some monster, but the truth is, he skipped town. Old Eddie had enough gray cells firing to figure out how to get out of town with everyone thinking he was dead."

Jane was shaking her head, "Oh, Clifford, Clifford, Clifford. You've got an answer for everything." She got the attention of the visitor and said, "Listen fella, would you ever believe a balloon with a month old cigar in his mouth? I love this old coot, but he's taking you for a ride."

"Sounds a bit odd, yeah, but you did go in and come out, right?" the golfer asked.

"Sure did. Here touch me. Want my autograph? Want your picture taken with me? I broke the myth. Trust me."

"Well, you're living proof that someone could go into the Triangle and come out so I guess I have to believe you." He pulled away and headed for the clubhouse to let people know what had happened.

"Now, don't you go thinking you're going to become a local folk hero, Clifford Hooker," Jane warned. "You're probably about to call some balladeer and ask for a song to be written about yourself."

"I wasn't, but that's a good idea. I might even be talking to Katie Couric on NBC in the morning."

"Well, if you do, throw out the cigar, brush your teeth, and make sure the camera gets you from the top of your head to your chin. Might as well put your best foot forward."

"May you 4-putt this green, my love!"

"I'm going to sink it to spite you. Notice the downward slope, Cliff. I wouldn't do much more than tap it." They both chuckled. Cliff and Jane didn't sound like they loved each other, but they really did. Jane sunk her putt for a birdie and Cliff 2-putted for a 7.

Within the next couple of hours, the news of Cliff's successful traipse into the forbidden Triangle did get around. People felt a bit relieved, because most truly believed that Eddie Hazard was dead in the Triangle and that his ghost would capture any other living thing that wandered in. Today, Cliff Hooker stood up to the myth and bravely walked into the Triangle. Three minutes later he stepped out with his Titleist and a surprise yet to be revealed.

When Cliff and Jane putted out on the 9th green, the TV station crew was there and so was a newspaper reporter. This was big news. The myth had been challenged and defeated. It was a story for all to read and hear about. The media would make sure it would be on the front page of tomorrow's paper and on the 6 p.m. news that evening. Surviving the Triangle was clearly Clifford Hooker's 15 minutes of fame.

The golf professional at Ghostly Links was Larry Ball. Larry was 31 years old, tanned, slim, light brown hair and today he was dressed in his usual slacks and a knit shirt with the country club's logo above the left pocket. He was not in the clubhouse when all of this attention was focused on Cliff Hooker. He was far from the clubhouse enjoying a round of golf with his fiancée, Brooke Parmore. Brooke was a private investigator who had a passion for golf as well as for solving difficult crimes.

Brooke was 29 years old, a few inches less than six feet tall. Her blond hair was pulled into a pony tail and swayed free from the opening in her visor which served to provide shade to her face with high cheek bones and a smile that charmed anyone glancing at her. She wore white shorts and a light blue blouse with a sleeveless sweater. White anklets presented a stark contrast to tanned legs. Her robin's egg blue golf glove matched the colors of her head covers and bag.

Larry and Brooke had become a couple over the past few years. When Brooke moved to the area from her home in England, she made it a priority to find the finest local golf course. She walked into the Ghostly Links Country Club to inquire about membership options. The first person she met was Larry, the golf pro. Larry would tell her often in the ensuing months that she was his "wish come true."

Brooke joined the country club and when she wasn't investigating a case, she could be found on the golf course. When Larry could break from his responsibilities he would join her, as was the case this afternoon. Normally he carried a cell phone so his assistant could reach him but on this day he left his phone in the clubhouse. A lot of commotion was going on in the clubhouse while he was enjoying a sub par round with Brooke who was only a few strokes above par herself.

✐

While Larry was hoping to sink a chip from the fringe of the 3rd green, Cliff answered each question factually and with confidence. Jane stood off to the side and kept shaking her head because she knew this was all going to go to Clifford's head and she'd have to live with his swollen dome. He would surely tell the story thousands of times and each time it would grow bigger and soon it would simply be too much to handle. But, she vowed at her wedding to love Cliff for better or worse, in sickness and in health, so she'd have to do her best to be supportive while keeping Clifford's head no bigger than an NBA basketball.

After a series of questions, the newspaper reporters were off to write their stories. The TV cameramen and reporters were quick to get back to the station to prepare reports that would surely have viewers talking about this event. Some would say that Cliff just got lucky, or that he didn't go in far enough, and that the Triangle remains alive and well. Others would tell friends and family that they never did fall for the myth of golfers disappearing in the Bermuda Triangle of the Links.

Clifford and Jane decided to play the back nine. They checked the scorecard before going to the 10th tee. Jane had carded a 37 on the first nine and Cliff recovered a bit with some lucky shots and carded a 45. Both had fairly good drives and second shots, but on the third shot, Cliff shanked it. The ball went to the bottom of a steep slope off to the right of the green. He told Jane to take the cart. He'd hit and walk.

"Walk to the green? Are you kidding?" Jane asked.

"Just a little hill."

"Listen. I'll wait for you with the cart. Your heart can't take a climb like that. I don't mind sharing your new found celebrity status because I love you in spite of your many faults. But, I'm not driving the cart back to the clubhouse with a dead Clifford Hooker. My goodness, what am I saying? I'd have to drag you in behind the cart if it had that much pulling power. I couldn't lift your leg into the cart let alone all 300 plus pounds of you."

"Oh, give me a break. I can handle it, Jane."

"Handle it? To you, that incline is Mt. Everest!"

"I'll meet you on the green, dead or alive!" Cliff said as he walked down to address his ball. Jane drove off shaking her head at the stubbornness of her husband.

Cliff chose his pitching wedge and lofted a perfect shot. The ball landed on the green and rolled up to within a foot of the hole. Jane clapped her hands and shouted, "Nice shot, Cliff! I hope you can get up here to see what a good shot that was!"

Cliff began to walk up the steep incline. Taking it one step at a time he arrived at the top of the hill. As he stepped onto the green, he said, "Well, if it isn't Jane Hooker. I see you made it to Heaven too. Guess I'm not surprised, living and loving me for so long, you've certainly earned your ticket. I'll bet you're surprised I made it though, aren't you?"

"Cliff, you are not even huffing and puffing. You can't go up three steps without breathing deep and asking your Maker for another day. You okay?"

"Yeah. Never felt better. It was a steep climb, but hey, I'm a strong guy."

"No, you're not, Cliff Hooker. Let me feel your pulse. It must be racing."

"No it isn't. I feel fine, really."

"Here, give me your wrist." Jane took several seconds trying unsuccessfully to find his pulse.

"See, the old ticker is so efficient you can't even find a pulse," Cliff replied, proud of his effortless climb.

"Let me listen to your heart, that is, if I can detect a beat from inside that thick and fat chest of yours."

Jane put her ear to his chest, but couldn't pick up a beat. She put her fingers to the side of Cliff's neck to feel his pulse. Again, she couldn't detect any rhythmic beat.

She stood back and looked him in the eye. *Maybe I'm looking at a ghost,* Jane thought.

"Cliff, is that you?" Jane said cautiously.

"What on earth are you talking about? Of course it's me. Who else would stand here in these silly looking knickers, tam-o'-shanter, and play golf with someone who constantly humiliates him?"

"What's the name of your grandson?" Jane asked, standing on the green.

"Grandson?" Cliff asked.

"The name of your grandson, our daughter's son. In Phoenix."

"Senior moment is all. His name is... . It's...."

"How old are you, Cliff?"

"How old am I? You know how old I am, you gave me a big party."

"Yeah, I know how old you are, I'm asking if you know how old you are."

"Well, let's see. I'm... I think I just turned... . Who cares how old I am? What's a number? Age is all attitude, you know that."

"Tap in that putt for your par, Cliff. I already 2-putted while you were walking up to the green. Let's get to the next tee."

During the ride to the 11th tee, Jane Hooker knew that her life was changed forever.

Chapter Two

Jane wanted to get home immediately, but Cliff was enjoying the round. He had some birdies and executed a few excellent shots. There was no reason to believe his luck wouldn't continue. "Why go home?"

"Because you have a heart that should be racing but isn't."

"Hogwash. I'm alive, taking your stinging comments and throwing some back. This is just like any other day. Who's got the honors, you or me?"

"Cliff, this is not like any other day. Something happened in the Triangle. You are not yourself. You don't have a heartbeat and you can't remember your grandson Philip's name."

"Yeah, Philip. That's it. Don't know how I could have allowed that to slip my mind. Yup, Philip's his name."

"And you couldn't remember that you are 63 years old."

"Right again, 63. That's it. Why would I want to remember that I'm 63, for cryin' out loud?"

"Well, guess playing in won't be a problem, but we're going to have Doctor Wedge take a look at your heart," Jane declared.

"Baloney. Why waste her time? I'll mention it at my checkup. Hey, do I look healthy or what?"

"Yes, you do, Cliff. I'll give you that. You've got the honors and even if you didn't, I'd yield to you for that fantastic chip shot."

Cliff hit his drive long and down the middle. Larry would have been proud to see his pupil follow directions to perfection. Jane teed off from the red markers and hit her usual straight shot positioning herself perfectly for her second shot. The rest of the round was typical. Jane carded a 40 and Cliff had a 43. During the round, Jane kept asking Cliff questions. In a nutshell, he didn't know his phone number, his address, his son's first name, and wasn't sure who was the president of the United States, and for that matter, didn't know there was a United States.

When they finished their round, Jane asked the ball boy to put their clubs away and to return the cart. She told Cliff to get in the car. They got off the course and out of the clubhouse area before anyone could stop him to talk about breaking the myth of the Bermuda Triangle of the Links.

No

Jane called Doctor Sara Wedge from her car phone. She got the receptionist. "Stacy? This is Jane Hooker. I need to talk to Dr. Wedge."

"She's with a patient right now, Jane."

"I'll hold."

"It could be awhile. How about if I have the doctor call you the moment she's free?"

"This is close to an emergency, Stacy. I'll hold."

"Well, in that case, I'll see if the doctor can be interrupted."

Dr. Wedge was soon on the phone. "What's the problem, Jane?"

"It's Cliff. I need you to see him right away. This must remain confidential."

"All of our interactions are confidential, that's no problem."

"This will challenge you, Sara. Please do whatever you can to fit Cliff in as soon as possible."

"Come right over to the office. I'll see him. Does he need to go to emergency, Jane?"

"No, he appears quite normal, but he's not. We'll be right over. I don't want anyone to see him but you."

"Well, the nurse will do a few routine things like weight, blood pressure and pulse."

"Absolutely not. The only one to look at Cliff must be you and with no one but me in the room."

"You sure have me curious here, Jane."

"Yes, I imagine I do. But, I'm serious and am desperately in need of your help. It will become very clear."

After Dr. Wedge hung up, she told her nurse to bring Mr. Hooker into an examination room as soon as he arrived, and she emphasized that there was not to be an intake procedure.

Dr. Wedge walked toward the examination room and wondered what this could be about. Often patients think something to be an emergency, only to find out that it is quite common. Such was undoubtedly the case with the Hookers, Dr. Wedge presumed.

About twenty minutes later the Hookers arrived at the doctor's office. They were escorted to examination room "B" without doing routine test procedures. Dr. Wedge entered the room.

"Good afternoon. Good to see you both."

"Thank you for seeing us so quickly," Jane said.

"Glad to help. What's the problem?" Dr. Wedge asked holding a rather thick chart.

"Cliff, who is this?" Jane asked.

"The doctor. What do you mean 'Who's this'? You think I'm an imbecile or something?"

"I know you know it's the doctor. But, what's the doctor's name?"

"Her name is …. I just can't bring it up right now. It'll come to me in a second."

Jane looked at Doctor Wedge. "You've been Cliff's doctor for twenty-five years; why you're practically family and he doesn't know who you are, Sara."

"Sara. Yeah, that's it," Cliff replied. "Right on the tip of my tongue. Sara, by golly. How ya doing?"

"I'm doing fine, Cliff. What brings you here today?"

"Jane brings me here, that's who. I'm doing fine, but she's all bent out of shape because I walked up a hill and didn't huff and puff. Sorry to bother you and take you away from really sick people, but you know Jane."

"He's got no heartbeat, Sara," Jane said, eager to drop the bombshell.

"No heartbeat?" Sara asked, astounded at what she had just heard.

"Find it then and when you do, let me listen."

Doctor Wedge put her stethoscope to his chest and listened carefully while moving the stethoscope from spot to spot. She took his wrist and sought a pulse. She put her fingers on his neck to feel the pulse there. Nothing.

"Please take off your shirt, Cliff."

Other than pounds and pounds of fat and some chest hair, nothing appeared to be out of the ordinary. She pushed and prodded here and there and when she applied some pressure to the left of his sternum, Cliff let out a howl. "Hey, hey, hey, that hurts, Doc!"

"Sorry, Cliff. Let me find that spot again. I won't apply any pressure." She found the spot and noted that it was tender. She looked a little closer and the area was slightly bruised.

"Well, Jane's right. There is not a heartbeat, but the blood is moving through your veins and arteries. I can't explain this. Can you?"

Cliff sat on the examining table and shook his head. Jane said, "Well, if you won't tell her, then I will. Cliff walked into the Triangle at the Ghostly Links Country Club this morning. He came out looking as he did when he went in. He thought he had broken the myth and was even interviewed on TV and by a newspaper reporter. On the 10th hole, he walked up a very steep incline. With his weight and heart condition, there was no way he could make it, let alone be breathing normally. Something was wrong and I didn't know if I was seeing a ghost or if Cliff was really standing on the 10th green."

"Hmmm, this is strange," Dr. Wedge said, puzzled.

"He didn't look like a ghost usually looks," Jane said. "I mean, you know, like a ghost looks like in the movies, sort of a white or a grey mist. The man was Cliff: looked like him, sounded like him, same old cantankerous overweight man that I love. But, in addition to not having a heartbeat, he didn't know how old he was, nor did he know his grandson's name."

"Something obviously happened in the Triangle," Sara said. "How long was he in there?"

"About five minutes," Jane replied.

"What do you remember, Cliff?"

"I walked in, pushing grass and brush left and right and then I guess I don't remember anything till I walked onto the course again. I had my Titleist ball with me and that's what I went in there to get."

"Same ball that you hit?"

"Yeah. I hit a Titleist Two. It's my lucky ball."

"So, you walked out with a Titleist Two?"

"Yeah. Here, I still have the ball in my pocket. I forgot to put it in my bag." Cliff handed the ball to Sara. She took it and turned to read the brand name. "This is a Titleist Four, Cliff."

"Hmmm, I could have sworn it was a Two."

"Did someone hand you the ball or did you find it in the Triangle?"

"I don't remember."

"Did you see anyone in the Triangle?"

"No. Nothin' but trees, brush, grass, very thick."

"You didn't see anyone and you didn't feel anyone do anything to you?"

"Nope. I was only in there a few minutes. What could anyone do in a few minutes?"

Sara looked at Cliff's back. She noticed a raised spot under his skin, just under his left shoulder blade. "Does this hurt, Cliff?"

"A little tender, yeah, but it doesn't hurt."

"I'd like to deaden this area and take a look at what is under your skin, Cliff. It feels like a postage stamp in size, but I don't know how thick it is nor do I know what it is."

"Yeah, I guess, if it won't hurt too much. Might as well find out what it is."

"Jane, I've got to have my assistant in here. I won't say anything to her. Is this okay with you?"

"Yes, sure."

The surgical procedure was performed after the area was deadened. Sara was able to examine the object, but couldn't free it as thin wires seemed to go deep into his body. She put it back, cleaned the area, and applied several stitches to the open wound. When the procedure was over, the assistant was asked to leave.

"I want to do an EKG on Cliff," Doctor Wedge said, needing to verify the lack of a heartbeat. She applied all the electrodes. The three watched the ink stylus go straight across the paper. "OK, now I need to bring my assistant back in for a chest x-ray. I can do this in my office and no one will see the film but the three of us."

The assistant returned and took the x-ray. After several minutes Sara returned with the film. "Well, let me tell you what I've found. There is no heart muscle in his chest. The small object in his back is a computer-like chip that somehow miraculously moves the blood along in his body. It simply flows like a stream that never stops. I can't explain the lack of memory. Something must have happened, but it appears that once you learn the fact, you have it. Right, Cliff?"

"I guess so," Cliff replied.

"Does that chip improve my putting and will it straighten out my drives?" Cliff asked with a chuckle. Jane and Sara were not smiling.

"I really don't know what happened," Dr. Wedge said, astonished at what she had discovered. "I mean, I know what I see, but I don't know why or how. It's beyond medical science."

"Well, what do we do now, Doctor?" Jane asked.

"I have no advice. I am shocked. Take it a day at a time and try to adjust, I suppose. Try your best to live a normal life, I guess."

"A normal life? Cliff has no heart, he can't recall thousands of facts, and you think we can live a normal life?" Jane responded.

"Well, of course not, but I mean, there doesn't seem to be anything that we can do to help Cliff. He continues to live and seems normal to me and to anyone who sees him."

"Nobody can find out about this or he'll be a freak! He'll be hounded by the media," Jane said fearfully. "We just want to be together, share zingers and play golf."

"Then do that. I promise I won't say a word and there will be nothing in Cliff's file to indicate what we've found today."

"What does he do to stay healthy?" Jane asked.

"Follow good eating and exercise habits. As of today, it looks like Cliff might live forever."

"Live forever? Almighty God, please save us from that possibility," Jane said sarcastically, but with a smile.

"Thanks, Jane," Cliff said, shaking his head. "May your ball find every pond on the course to its liking."

"Well, sounds like you two are back to normal already," Doctor Wedge said with a smile. "Jane, you'll have to become a school teacher and home school this rather bright man," Doctor Sara said, patting them both on their shoulders.

While the Hookers were meeting with their doctor, Larry and Brooke completed their round of golf. As soon as Larry went into the pro shop, his assistant briefed him about Cliff Hooker's walk into the Triangle and all of the commotion it caused. *This is all I need,* Larry thought. He escorted Brooke to her convertible, gave her a kiss on the cheek and told her he'd see her again soon. Before Brooke got into her car, Larry said, "You're going to hear about a man who walked into the Triangle today. Apparently the media got wind of it. I can tell you right now; this thing will escalate into a major headache for me."

"Do you want me to investigate this and put an end to speculation and rumor?" Brooke asked. "If we could find out what happens to people, we could put it to bed. Over time the mystique of the Triangle would become a thing of the past."

"Thanks. Let's let it ride for now."

"I'd be glad to look into it, Larry."

"I appreciate it, Brooke. I'll keep your offer in my back pocket. I'll see you later."

Brooke smiled, gave him a hug and drove away.

The missing heart phenomenon was intriguing to Dr. Wedge. Sara had a couple of patients whose hearts were in bad condition. They were on lists for heart transplants but were high-risk. She feared that when their name came up, they would most likely learn that the risk of death in surgery was too great. Dr. Wedge couldn't help but entertain the thought that a step into the Bermuda Triangle of the Links would be the perfect cure for her patients and for the price of losing memory of facts, life may be assured. In a matter of seconds, she dismissed the idea because it was fraught with malpractice suits.

Sara felt an obligation to let the pro at Ghostly Links know that it was still not safe to go into the Triangle. She called him and let him know that while she couldn't give any particulars, she felt that the warnings and the legal signatures concerning entering at your own risk should be maintained.

"While I have you on the line, Doctor, may I tell you something?" Larry asked.

"Yes, definitely."

"Eddie Hazard was the first to enter the Triangle and that was the day the course opened six years ago. He has never been back, but I correspond on occasion with his son, Eric. Eric tells me that his father, since walking into and out of the triangle, seems to be full of energy and life. He almost became a new man."

"Really? Does Eddie live in the area?"

"No, he moved to California. He wanted a new life. He got himself a Harley-Davidson, dates women decades younger than he is, plays 27 holes of golf on most days, and I think he even signed up for the Ironman Triathlon in Hawaii next year."

"Can I contact Eric?"

"I don't think he'd mind if I gave you his phone number or address."

"I'd like his e-mail address if you have that."

"I do. His e-mail address is cantkeepupwithmyoldman @yahee.com"

"Got it, thanks."

"Say, Doc, do you know something about the Triangle?" Larry asked.

"I believe that there is a connection between the Triangle, the strange noises the golfers hear, the unexplained ball movement on the course, and the sightings of ghosts. I suspect that something happens in your forbidden Triangle that we may not understand.

"Now, having heard what Eric has said about his father, I think it important that people remain warned about the Triangle. It's your property and your policy. I shouldn't be meddling in what is none of my business. If I were you, it would be my policy that no person goes into the Triangle. But, human nature being what it is, you can't really control it."

"Thank you, Doctor. We'll do our best to maintain our policy," Larry said.

"Good, but then again, it could be that good things happen in the Triangle. After listening to what happened to Eddie, your Triangle could be the long, lost, fountain of youth."

Chapter Three

Friday, August 19, 2005
Ghostly Links Country Club

A week after Cliff's walk into the Triangle, the city's religious leaders had their bimonthly golf league meeting. It was called the "I've Been Called to the Links League." It was the closest thing to an ecumenical council imaginable. Almost every denomination in the city was represented. The league members told each other jokes that would bring a gold mine to a comedy club owner. It seemed that Golf, not God, was the force that brought all of these different minds together.

A member of the Ghostly Links Country Club once suggested that a writer follow the group for a month or so because a religious humor book could easily be written. Most of the jokes could only be shared among the group. As much as the men and women of the cloth wanted to share the humor with their congregations, they just couldn't do it.

The "I've Been Called to the Links League" was a 9-hole league, as most members felt guilty taking a few hours from their ministerial duties to have some fun. But, all agreed that the break gave them a much needed opportunity to get their minds off the stress and strains of running a church, parish, or synagogue.

While on the putting green, some of the league members began talking about Cliff Hooker's breaking the myth of the Triangle.

Father James McDuffy said, "Good example of faith, if you ask me."

"Example of faith, Jim?" Reverend Chip Hogan, the minister of the Baptist Church, replied. "It's more an example of being a fool."

"Well, he believed he would survive and acted on that faith, so it seems to me that what he did was a good example of faith," Father Jim replied. "We're always asking followers of Jesus to trust in Him, to have faith and to be more Christ-like."

"You're not suggesting that Cliff Hooker is someone our faithful should emulate, I hope?" Chip asked.

"Whoa, I wouldn't go that far," chuckled Father McDuffy. "I'm simply saying this is an example of a man following his faith."

"Faith in what, you must make that clear. Faith in God? Heaven forbid, Jim!"

"Faith that he would not be harmed by challenging the Triangle. That's all I'm trying to say."

On the other side of the putting green the Methodist minister and the Presbyterian minister were having a dollar-a-putt contest. One dollar for each putt sunk longer than 10 feet. At the moment, the Methodist led the Presbyterian by three dollars.

Everyone in the 27-member league was present for the shotgun start on the front nine. Well, everyone except Rabbi Cupski. He called to say that his biggest contributor at the Synagogue was having a bunion removed and he felt his place was with the family at the hospital. He promised to join the group next time.

At exactly 8:30 in the morning, one golfer at each of the nine holes hit a ball to begin the day of league play. As fate would have it, the twosome of Father McDuffy and Reverend Hogan, playing without Rabbi Cupski, sliced their balls horrifically into the Triangle.

As they pulled their carts along the 8th fairway and walked in the direction of the Triangle, Reverend Chip said, "Well,

Father, are you going to act on your faith?"

"Act on my faith that I won't come out alive?"

"No, on the faith that you'll be just fine when you come out."

"Well, I'm not so sure I'll be fine when I come out, if I come out."

"But what a story to tell your parishioners at next weekend's Masses," Chip Hogan replied, almost challenging Father McDuffy to walk in. "It would show that you conquered your fear and walked out victorious. Jesus faced fear and showed his power over sin and evil. You can do the same and they'll love you for it, Jim. Your homily could be your best ever! The collection plates could overflow and boy wouldn't that help with the new gym you want built."

"It sure would. Hmm, I might do it," Father McDuffy said, pondering the possibility. "You going to join me? You're leading me into temptation and I want to know if you're willing to practice what you preach? Are you coming in with me, Chip?"

"Are you nuts? Of course not. I've got a family. You don't have a family, Jim. What have you got to lose?"

"My parish is my family, Chip. Tending the flock takes all my time."

"Well, we either play a provisional or go into the Triangle and see what happens. What will it be?" Chip asked.

"I'll tell you what. If I go in and come out, you'll come to my church for weekend Mass and explain to all that you made a big mistake in not becoming a Catholic, but that you seek forgiveness and will cheer for Notre Dame for at least the next 10 years."

"You've got a deal!" Chip replied.

Father Jim countered, "I'll tell you what, if you go in with me, I'll go to one of your services and say that I erred in not becoming a Baptist, and I will promise to get married the first chance I get. How is that?"

"It's a deal. Are we going in together or one at a time?" Chip asked.

"Together. That way we can help each other if harm does seem to be lurking in our path."

"OK. You sure you want to do this, Father? Do we need to say a prayer first?"

"I'm not going to bother God with such foolishness. We're only going in to get a golf ball; after all, Cliff Hooker broke the myth. This is no big deal. But, before we go in, no crossed fingers. Going in and coming out will cause us to visit each other's church next Sunday and we both agree to follow through on our promises."

"Exactly. OK, we going in?" Chip asked.

"Sure. What have we got to lose?"

Each golfer took an iron to help part the brush and grass and then each stepped over the imaginary boundary between the rough and the Triangle.

When Reverend Carolyn Spiker of the Episcopal Church, Reverend Troy Gripley of the Church of the Nazarene, and Missy Wilson, the Choir Director of the Church of Christ stepped onto the 8th tee, they couldn't see the twosome up ahead.

"Hmmm, they should be on the green by now. It's only a par-4 and we just finished a par-3," Carolyn said, a bit concerned.

"Isn't that a couple of pull carts over in the right rough?" Missy said, pointing toward the Triangle.

"Yeah, looks like it. You only get five minutes to look for a lost ball and if that's what they were doing, looking for their drives, they should've moved on. They wouldn't want to be holding us up or the whole league for that matter."

"Well, let's go ahead and hit. They might let us play through," Troy said. "You're up, Missy; you had a birdie back there. A nice birdie, I might add."

The three hit their drives and began walking down the 8th fairway.

"Are those guys ever coming out?" Missy asked.

"Of course not, not if they went in, that's the Bermuda Triangle of the Links," Troy replied. "I can't believe they'd be so foolish as to tempt fate with going in there for a golf ball."

"Well, let's go over there and see what we can see," Carolyn said.

They did and saw nothing except two pull carts with the 3-iron missing from each bag. They didn't hear anything either.

"What shall we do? Shall we go in and try to find them?" Troy asked.

"I try to be my brother's keeper, but there's no way I'm crossing that line," Missy replied. "If they're OK, they'll be out soon. If they're not OK, I don't want to be in there with them!"

"But maybe they need help," Carolyn said. "They're our friends. We'd stop on the highway if they had an accident. What's the difference? I gave a sermon on the Good Samaritan last Sunday. If I don't go in, I'll be a hypocrite. I'd never want my congregation to hear about my not being willing to help out my fellow man."

"Well, I didn't give a sermon on the good Samaritan," Troy countered. "I gave one on following your instinct after asking God to help in a difficult situation. My instinct tells me to stay outside this Triangle!"

"I'm with you," Missy said, emphatically.

"Well, I have to at least step in and see if I can see them," Carolyn said.

"OK, don't go far and cry out if you need any help," Missy begged.

"I shouldn't have any trouble," Carolyn replied. "That guy Cliff, what's his name, went in and came out OK last week. I'll just look for them and be right out."

Carolyn stepped into the Triangle and disappeared. Missy said, "Oh my God, we've lost her!" In about three minutes Carolyn stepped outside and looked toward Missy and Troy.

"Thank God you're back!" Missy exclaimed.

"Back from where?" Carolyn asked.

"Back from where? Back from the Triangle. You went in to look for Father Jim and Reverend Chip," Missy explained.

"Who are Father Jim and Reverend Chip?"

"Whoa boy, this is going to be hard to explain," Troy said, shaking his head.

"Carolyn, do you know who you are, or where you are, or who you are with?" Missy asked.

Carolyn seemed to be in a trance as she looked around. "No, I don't know you. Should I? And, I don't know where I am, but it looks like a golf course. Do I play golf?"

"Your name is Carolyn Spiker. You are the priest at the

Episcopal Church in town and yes, you play golf. As a matter of fact, you're quite good," Troy said. Carolyn simply listened.

"I think we need to get off the course and get to a hospital," Missy suggested. "Carolyn needs help and we need to also explain that Father Jim and Reverend Chip are missing in the Triangle." Troy agreed. The three walked ahead pulling their own clubs, plus the clubs belonging to Jim and Chip.

❦

Once more the Bermuda Triangle of the Links at the Ghostly Links Country Club was in the news. But this time, it was about two missing clergymen and a "survivor," as Carolyn was referred to by a news reporter. The public learned that Reverend Spiker remained under observation at a local hospital.

The doctor came out of the examination room and sat down with Carolyn's parents, Missy, and the head of the leadership council of the local Episcopal Church.

"I've thoroughly examined Carolyn," the doctor began. "We've run several tests on her including a variety of blood tests, an EKG, X-rays, and an MRI. I also asked our resident psychiatrist to join me to do a preliminary evaluation. Let me get right to the point. I'm sorry if this may disturb you, but, Carolyn Spiker is not with us."

Her parents gasped. "Not with us, what do you mean?" her mother asked, bringing her hands to her mouth with fear showing in her eyes.

"I'm sorry, but the woman in that examination room is not Carolyn Spiker. We had her dental records checked. The pattern of her bite does not match her dental records. She has no memory of who she is. X-rays in her file are not revealing the same bone structure."

"But, she looks like Carolyn!" her mother exclaimed, clinging to some hope that her daughter was going to be OK.

"I'm sorry, Mrs. Spiker, but Carolyn is not that woman, not physically, emotionally, cognitively or even spiritually. I'm not saying your daughter is dead, I'm only saying that the woman in my examination room is not Carolyn Spiker, that's all I'm saying."

"Well, then we need to get into the Triangle and try to find her."

"I don't recommend that, Mrs. Spiker," the doctor quickly replied. "You'll have to work with the police to find your daughter."

"What will happen to the woman in the examination room?" Carolyn's father asked.

"I'm not certain. I'll contact our social worker and we'll handle that here at the hospital."

Carolyn's friends gathered in a circle, put their arms around one another, and prayed for Carolyn Spiker, and for the stranger.

The doctor who had examined Carolyn left the shocked family and walked down the hospital corridor. He opened the door to the examination room. It was empty. There was no evidence of a woman having been in the room. The paper on the examination table was not wrinkled. There was no writing on the intake form and nothing written on the doctor's report form.

At first, the doctor was certain that he had mistakenly entered the wrong room. He checked each room and found that he had entered the correct room. But, the impossible had just happened before his eyes. Now there was no evidence that he had examined anyone. He even lifted the top on the wastebasket to find the waste materials from his evaluation. Nothing. Surely, maintenance had cleaned the room. He checked. Maintenance hadn't come into the area. He held up the film from the X-rays — blank. He checked for the readout of the EKG. It was clear of any ink. There was absolutely no evidence of anyone being in the room or any tests being done within the last hour.

❦

The authorities believed it important to contact people in Father Jim's life and in Reverend Chip's life as well. The police chief called Bishop Walker and explained that Father McDuffy had apparently gone into the Triangle that morning and was missing.

"I've got some news for you, Chief," the Bishop said, joyfully.

"Good or bad?"

"Good. Father McDuffy is sitting in my office."

"He is?"

"Yes, he has just confessed to spending time on a golf course when the sheep of his flock needed to be tended to," the Bishop said with a chuckle.

"Does he seem okay to you?" the Chief asked.

"No, to be honest he doesn't."

"In what way?"

"Well, he's telling me he made a promise to Reverend Hogan that he would go to the Baptist church this Sunday and say that he wishes he was a Baptist and that he would get married as soon as possible. He's asking not only for forgiveness but for advice as to how to get out of this mess."

"Hmm, I don't know anything about that," the Chief said, thinking the Bishop was merely bringing some humor to a frightening situation.

"I regret telling you this, Chief. At least you're not a reporter from some tabloid who would blab this all over the country. It will be embarrassing enough for us in the Diocese without it getting on the AP wire."

"Again, Bishop, are you absolutely certain that the man in your office is Father McDuffy?" the Chief asked.

"As sure as I'm sitting here talking to you, Father McDuffy is in my office. Yes."

"Will you do me one favor?"

"Sure."

"Ask him to tell you the name of the pope."

"Hang on. Jim, what's the name of the pope?"

"Pope? Her name is...? Guess I'm not sure. Should I know?" Father Jim asked.

Bishop Walker was stunned and that put it mildly. He needed to save face so he said, "Yeah, he got it, Chief. He said, 'John Paul the Second.'" The Bishop's heart was beating at a fast pace and even skipping a beat every now and then.

"That's good. Glad to hear it, Bishop."

"You think he's crazy or something, Chief? Every priest knows the name of the pope, we all work for him."

"I know, just curious, that's all. OK, glad he got it right. Won't bother you anymore. You've got work to do. Bye."

The Bishop hung up the phone and looked Father McDuffy in the eye. "James McDuffy, are you crazy? Of course you should know who the pope is for Christ's sake! Whoops, forgive me, Lord," the Bishop said, lifting his eyes heavenward. "He's the head of the church, Jim. Did you get hit on the head on that course this morning?"

"Don't think so," Father McDuffy replied. "By the way, who is Reverend Hogan?"

❧

After conversing with the Bishop, the chief of police called the Baptist Church.

"First Baptist Church. How may I help you?" a pleasant voice answered.

"This is the police department calling. Tell me, who's in charge when Reverend Hogan is not around?"

"That would be me, his secretary. I run this place. My biggest job is making the Reverend think he does. How can I help you?"

"Well, he walked into the Bermuda Triangle of the Links over at the Ghostly Links Country Club this morning and we're trying to locate him."

"Well, I'll be. He told me he was off to visit folks who were sick and dying. Now, I find out he meant to see the 'sick of work' and 'the dying to play golf' folks."

"Has the Reverend stopped in within the last couple of hours?"

"Nope. It's been quiet around here."

"Do you expect him soon?"

"He better be here. He's got an appointment this afternoon at 3:00."

"If he shows up, we'd like to know about it. Can you give me a call?"

"Going to feel a little strange calling the police to report that Reverend Hogan has arrived for work. He's not into some drug ring or being investigated for smuggling cigarettes from Canada, or God forbid being at the Casino?"

"Not that we know about, but if any of those come to light, we'd appreciate your passing that information along as well."

"I'll give you a call the moment I see him."
"Thanks."

❦

Early in the afternoon the law enforcement authorities got involved. They sent up a helicopter to look at the Triangle from the air. They had a heat sensor device to see if a human might be in the thick and heavy brush below, but it gave no such indication. These efforts were also done when Eddie Hazard turned up missing.

The police would've interviewed Carolyn Spiker, but there was no one to interview. The reporters went to the parish chancery to talk to Father Jim, but he wasn't there. In fact, no one had seen Father Jim since the Bishop claimed he was in his office the afternoon of the infamous walk into the Triangle. Chip was still missing.

One reporter did try to contact Cliff Hooker, but Jane was very protective and made sure that nobody conversed with Cliff, and she meant nobody. The famous couldn't get through. Larry King was denied. The producer of *60 Minutes* was denied. Barbara Walters and Connie Chung had no luck. David Letterman and Jay Leno didn't even have their phone calls returned.

❦

Dr. Wedge sent an e-mail to Eric Hazard. It read, "Mr. Hazard. I was given your e-mail address by golf professional Larry Ball of the Ghostly Links Country Club. He told me about your father and his healthy life style. I'm a physician and am curious. Can you tell me anything about his experience in the Triangle? Has he been examined by a doctor? I am hoping you can help me, Mr. Hazard."

Sara clicked on the "Send" button and within a minute she heard "You've Got Mail."

The message was from Eric. With high hopes, she read, "Dr. Wedge, I am sorry, but I am not willing to discuss my father's experience at Ghostly Links. He wishes his privacy maintained and I will honor his request. My father is a healthy gentleman and for that we are thankful. I trust you will understand. Eric Hazard."

After e-mailing Dr. Wedge, Eric called Larry Ball.

"Sounds like folks are getting stirred up around that Triangle."

"Yup, lots of attention lately."

"Dad doesn't want to come out of the closet, so to speak, so I'm doing everything I can to keep him isolated."

"I understand," Larry said. "I gave a doctor your e-mail address and trust that was okay?"

"Sure. I didn't give her any help. Dad wants his privacy and I will honor it."

"I understand. The doctor seemed sincere and gave me the impression that she was interested in looking into the mystery, at least from a health perspective."

"No problem giving her my address. Normally, I'd be cooperative, but not about Dad. You understand, don't you, Larry?"

"Absolutely. Your dad makes the Triangle sound like the fountain of youth, which for him, I guess it was. I'll tell you this, if the media ever told the country that the Fountain of Youth was at Ghostly Links, I'd be up to my neck with people all clamoring to get into that small plot of land.

"Yeah, you'd undoubtedly have senior citizens lined up for miles. They'd come in charter buses like they're heading for the casinos."

"You got that right."

"Dad's living proof that that Triangle you've got there gives you a whole new lease on life," Eric said.

"Well, it's America and your dad can have privacy if he wants. If he changes his mind and wants to talk about the Triangle, please give me a warning. I'll charge a thousand bucks a person to enter the Triangle and then live the rest of my days in Maui!"

"I'll warn you for sure, but right now he's kicking up his heels so much that I don't think he's got any interest in causing folks to go to Ghostly Links like they did to that *Field of Dreams* place in Iowa."

Chapter Four

Friday, August 26, 2005

A week had passed since the clergy golf league had their experience at the Triangle. In addition to remaining isolated, Cliff Hooker had lost weight. His exercise put no strain on his missing heart. His body was burning fat like a hot furnace. He lost weight so fast that Dr. Wedge was quite concerned about the effect of the quick weight loss on the rest of his body.

Cliff learned facts at the rate of a genius; so almost within a few days, his brain had him back to where he was when he went into the Triangle. Jane didn't want any attention, so she didn't report that their home was simply not the same after the Triangle episode. Doors opened without someone being on either side. Cliff would jokingly say they were his friends and he asked forgiveness for their lack of manners. Crazy things happened like appliances going on and off at will. Cliff claimed that his friends were experimenting with modern living conveniences. He would always laugh when making these statements, so Jane thought he was just making light of a stressful situation.

❧

Jane did not tell Cliff that she had made appointments with a psychiatrist and their lawyer. She talked to the psychiatrist about her state of mental health living with a man who had no heart and in a home that seemed to be inhabited by ghosts. Jane had a sense of humor and she loved Cliff. But, the man who came out of the Triangle was not the man who went in. Living with Cliff was like adjusting to a new man, and not just any man, but a man who brought ghosts into their home.

Jane did a lot of talking at her first session with the doctor. The psychiatrist gave Jane credit for adapting, but could tell that the stress and strain on her was a bit more than a normal person could handle. He was concerned, offered a little practical advice, and prescribed a relaxant to get through these stressful times.

Jane visited their lawyer later that afternoon. She shared in confidence the same information she had shared with her psychiatrist. Her concern was twofold: in the event that she would decide to leave Cliff, what steps would need to be taken to protect herself, and secondly, was there any precedence for settling an estate with a ghost?

The attorney realized that he was facing a whole new arena in his practice. He could help with advice concerning the possible separation and divorce, but representing a client married to a ghost, would be different, and that put it mildly.

Jane went home in a daze. She didn't really know the man she was living with and she was thinking of getting a divorce. Of course, she was troubled by Cliff's not being himself, but she was also troubled by the ghosts.

When Jane got home, she went into the living room and there nailed to the wall, was a Crucifix. Jane and Cliff were not Catholic nor was anybody in their family. There was no way that religious symbol could have gotten into their home from the outside. This time Cliff didn't claim a friend was responsible. But every time Jane took it down and hid it, it would mysteriously reappear on the living room wall.

Jane stood in front of the Crucifix, lowered her head and prayed silently. *Oh Lord, please don't have tears fall or blood ooze from you. If that would get out, people would be lined up in front of my home for weeks and months to see or simply to be near where You cried or bled. I'll try to adjust to your being on the wall, but please, Lord, don't cry or bleed. I simply can't handle it. Amen.*

The last thing Jane was going to do was to tell anyone, besides her psychiatrist and attorney, that her home was being inhabited by ghosts. Once again, the media, which she feared with a passion, would have a feeding frenzy.

Jane talked to Cliff about her possibly leaving and starting a new life. This greatly disturbed Cliff and for the first time in quite awhile, he openly wept and showed genuine emotion and fear. Jane felt compassion for him and realized that the change was perhaps as difficult for Cliff as it was for her.

Jane and Cliff turned inward. They didn't go anywhere, ever. They became hermits in their home and eventually closed themselves off from people completely. They didn't answer the door or phone, and even wore disguises to get food at the grocery store. Cliff created an in-home gym, and he simply began to become a shell of his old self.

Brooke Parmore was a member of the Catholic Church where Father Jim was the pastor. She had come to the States from England about five years ago. Brooke's skills as a detective were exceptional. She had worked for Scotland Yard, but had wanderlust in her soul and wanted to explore the world while she was young. She thought she'd live in the States for about five years and then move on to some other place for another five. But, she fell in love with Larry Ball.

The Bishop had sent a letter to the parish acknowledging that Father Jim was out of town and outlined the circumstances around his being gone. He explained that because of the shortage of priests he could not permanently assign a priest to the parish, but a priest from a neighboring community would come over for a Mass on Sunday. He asked all parishioners to try and band together to help one another until he could assign a priest to the parish.

Some of the people in the church knew of Brooke's reputation in crime investigation. They approached her and asked her to become involved. They said that they couldn't pay her much, but they would be indebted to her if she could solve this mystery. Father Jim was loved and respected. The people of the parish thought they should support some effort to try and solve the mystery around Ghostly Links.

Brooke Parmore would only accept the challenge if Larry would agree to her getting involved. She had no experience with ghosts and haunted places, but she knew that castles in her native England had stories to tell.

Brooke's first step was to contact Larry. She drove to the country club and found him in the Pro Shop ordering some equipment. She told him of the request of people in her church to try and solve the mystery.

"I guess it would be a good idea for you to get involved now," Larry replied. "If anyone is going to get involved, I'd just as soon it be you."

"I'll only look into it if you agree, Larry. I don't want to bring any more attention to this thereby causing you any grief. I love you and I don't want to create problems or be in the way."

"No, that's not it. I just think that a lot of attention around here won't be good for the members who have a right to come to their club and play without a lot of curious people coming in and out, that's all."

"So, do I have a green light?"

"I guess so. I'm more afraid of what you will learn."

"Afraid of what I might learn?" Brooke asked, perplexed.

"Yeah, you know when all is said and done, it might be better to leave well enough alone."

"It's your call, honey," Brooke said.

"I think it needs to be solved. Yes, you have a green light and I'll help with whatever you need to be successful."

❦

Once Larry had agreed to have Brooke investigate, she contacted the law enforcement authorities in the city where she was known and respected. The police had a strong feeling about keeping private detectives at a distance, but the beauty of Miss Parmore gave her license to talk with the authorities and to wiggle her way into cases when other private investigators would be told to keep their distance.

Brooke talked at great length with the local chief of police, Todd Flagg, who decided to share his information. He went over his conversations with Reverend Hogan's secretary and with the Bishop. Chief Flagg had explained the work of his officers and basically let her know that this was out of his league. Unless a crime was committed, he really didn't want to be involved. "Let well enough alone," seemed to be Todd's motto.

If Brooke wanted to carry the ball with this, it was fine with the police department. Of course it was understood that any investigation of crime was their responsibility and Chief Flagg would not need any help from Brooke Parmore. But, lacking a crime, she was given his blessing. The chief offered to help should any resources of the city police be needed. Brooke thanked Chief Flagg for his information and his support. She'd keep him informed.

Next Brooke began to do some research into the paranormal. She wasn't a disbeliever, but neither was she one to get enthused with a report of a ghost sighting. In general, she believed that these sightings were all explainable, which most of them had proven to be. But, she had an open mind and if this case involved ghosts, strange sounds, and unexplained movements and such, so be it. She knew it would broaden her experience as a private investigator and if nothing else, would give her party conversation to last a lifetime.

Brooke contacted Dr. Luciano DiNatale, a world-renowned authority on paranormal experiences. Dr. DiNatale had been making a name for himself at the Center for Extracelestial Studies based at the University of New Jersey. Luciano published scholarly papers and hosted a number of seminars on the subject of the supernatural. Brooke had met him at one of his conferences. A female friend wanted a companion for a conference where Luciano was the keynote speaker, so Brooke went along. She attended the social functions as well as a session or two.

Luciano was a distinguished older man. He had a full head of wavy, dark hair, was clean-shaven, and was exceptionally handsome. He did remember Brooke. "How can I help the beautiful investigator?" he asked when Brooke called.

"Believe it or not, I've been asked to look into a case that might have some connection to ghosts and strange phenomenon. I learned a long time ago that to be successful you need to surround yourself with people who can help you. I think you can help me."

"I'm sure I can. This wouldn't happen to involve the golf course they call Ghostly Links would it?"

"Yes, as a matter of fact it does. How would you know?" Brooke asked surprised that Luciano would know about the case.

"I may be an academician, but I do watch *CNN* and I do read *USA Today* on occasion. And, I certainly stay up-to-date with anything that involves the paranormal. I also play golf, so put all those together and you can understand why the place has my interest."

"You play golf, do you?" Brooke asked.

"Oh, yes. I am quite taken with the sport, actually. Next to beautiful women, golf is my passion. I simply don't have the time to play often."

"Well, what would it take to get you to come out here for a round of golf and some discussion of this case?"

"Dinner and an evening in your presence would be all I would need."

"Well, aren't you a charmer," Brooke replied.

"It's true. You are the most beautiful woman I've ever seen."

"Thank you for the compliment. Flying here from New Jersey is a long way to come for dinner, but I do need your experience and your knowledge. I would sincerely appreciate you joining me on this case, Doctor."

"I'd be happy to, Miss Parmore. Assuming I can get flights tomorrow, I should arrive late afternoon or early evening."

"Wonderful. Thank you very much," Brooke said.

"You are most welcome. I will bring my clubs if you think we'll have enough time to play."

"Well, I would hope so. I don't know how this case will unravel, but I am hoping we can play a round or two. My fiancée Larry Ball is the club pro and he would welcome you to a very challenging course."

"I'll bring my clubs. I'll take a cab or rent a car and check into a hotel. May I take you and Mr. Ball to dinner?" Luciano asked.

"Thank you."

"You pick a delightful place."

"We like to go to the English Inn. I think you will enjoy it."

"Fine."

"Oh, could you please bring along some resource material on the paranormal?" Brooke asked.

"As you speak I am thinking of some literature and case studies that might pertain to this interesting case."

Brooke suggested Luciano stay at the Radisson Hotel, and offered to book him a room. He accepted.

"I'll greet you at the Radisson tomorrow evening at eight o'clock," Brooke said before saying good-bye.

Brooke was off to a good start. She had Larry's support, the support of the local police chief, and she was able to interest an international expert on the paranormal from the East coast.

Brooke noticed early on that there was a form of life that didn't seem to be impacted, nor influenced, by the Triangle. She noticed a hawk perched in a tree. She saw a chipmunk scurry into the Triangle and within seconds scamper back out and seemed to be fine. She asked Larry about other animals that might go into and out of the Triangle.

"I've seen some deer come out, but really, I've never kept track. No one has ever asked about the animals. I guess that's because we've never seen any dead animals out on the course."

"I guess it would be safe to conclude that birds and animals are free from the effects of the Triangle," Brooke hypothesized. "Unless, they too became ghostly."

"The only difference would be that as far as we know, nobody missed one. There is no animal media to cover anything different or unusual," Larry replied with a smile. Brooke chuckled at the thought.

But, she felt it should be tested. She didn't want to come under the slings and arrows of an animal rights group, but she wanted an animal to go in and come out and then be checked over by a veterinarian. She didn't want to knowingly put a harmless animal into a spooky environment, but for some reason, she needed to know if the effects of the Triangle were limited to humans.

Brooke went to the dog pound, explained her problem and why she needed an animal for an experiment. She stated quite convincingly that she felt quite sure no harm would come to the animal. A dog was volunteered for the experiment. She said she would bring him back as soon as she was finished.

After asking a vet to check out the dog, Brooke and the black lab headed for the golf course. She named the dog Lucky because she thought him lucky to be given some freedom from the kennel to run and fetch as he was bred to do. She explained to Larry Ball that she wanted Lucky to go into the Triangle and come back out. Larry thought it a bit silly, but said the experiment was fine with him.

Brooke took a stick and walked with the black lab to the Triangle along the rough of the ninth hole. She threw a stick a few times so Lucky could get the idea of what was expected. It was great fun and the retriever went after the stick each time, undoubtedly due to instinct. After Brooke threw the stick, and as soon as Lucky picked it up, she'd whistle and shout "Bring it here, Lucky. Bring it here."

Nobody was playing the ninth hole when the detective and dog went out for some fun. Toss and retrieve, toss and retrieve, and then Brooke threw the stick into the Triangle. Lucky jumped into the brush and tall grass. When he didn't come right out, Brooke thought it was because he was looking for the stick. She waited and then shouted, "Bring it here, Lucky. Bring it here!" Lucky didn't appear.

In about five minutes, the dog came out of the Triangle with a stick in his mouth. It was a different one, but it was a stick. Brooke hooked a leash to his collar and off they went to see the veterinarian.

She pulled up, parked her car, and led Lucky into the vet's office. The vet picked him up, set him on the table, checked him out and said, "This dog is the same dog I checked out an hour ago. No changes that I can tell. His heart sounds good. He's alert and seems just as healthy as when he left with you."

"Good. I'm glad to hear that."

"You going to take him to the pound?" the vet asked.

"You know, let me ask you, is he going to be put to sleep if I don't keep him?"

"As I understand it, he's been there quite a while with no takers. It will be relatively soon, I fear. I don't make those decisions so I don't know, but after awhile they have to go."

"Lucky is coming home with me," Brooke said with conviction. "Any dog willing to sacrifice, even if unknowingly, has a right to live. He's my dog now. Okay with you, Lucky?" Lucky began to pant and wag his tail. It was as if he knew he had just been given a long life. Perhaps, if he had had the capacity to wish, his wish may have come true.

Brooke continued to watch her new companion carefully, trying to note any change in behavior. She didn't know him well, but he continued to behave as he always had, even if "always" meant less than a day.

∞

Whack! The ball left the tee with a massive amount of energy. It pierced the light mist now falling over Ghostly Links. John Score had tagged another ball that would go at least 300 yards. He was the Tiger Woods of Ghostly Links. He often won the club championship and could hit the long ball. His problem was putting.

Larry Ball often said that if John Score could putt, he'd be on the tour. He'd almost invariably be going for eagle on a par-5 and birdies on most other holes, but nine times out of ten, he'd simply par the hole. His handicap was zero, but in this day and age, you needed to do better than that to have a future as a touring pro.

John Score was the reigning amateur at Ghostly Links Country Club. Everyone who played Ghostly Links or who looked at the plaque listing the club champions over the past six years knew it.

John Score's son Lloyd was about seven years old. John would allow his son to go along with him whenever he played. To keep Lloyd busy, he gave him a ball retriever. Lloyd would retrieve balls from creeks, ponds, the woods. He would take them home, clean them and sell them to golf driving ranges, or he would take the good balls and sell them to his dad's friends at discount prices. He was quite a businessman at a young age.

Lloyd had been lectured since the day he set foot on the course as a four-year-old that the Triangle was off limits. He received a lecture as stern as the one he got from his mother whenever he happened near the road in front of his home. In fact, it was rare that Lloyd even set foot in the rough by the Triangle.

A week ago, John had told Lloyd that he could be trusted to go up to the Triangle, but could never go past the line that separates the rough from the Triangle. Lloyd listened and heeded his father's stern warning.

"But, if I see a ball in the Triangle, can I reach in with my retriever and scoop it out?" Lloyd asked.

"I guess so, but listen to me, son. You must never step into that area. Am I making myself clear?" Lloyd nodded, and knew that whatever was inside the wooded area was dangerous.

His father's playing partner hit his ball in the rough by the Triangle on the first hole. The three went over to find it and while his father and partner walked along the edge of the Triangle, Lloyd spotted what appeared to be a brand new ball within reach of his extended ball retriever. The ball was under a leaf and only a young and perfect eye, such as belonged to the young Lloyd Score, would have spotted it.

Lloyd extended his retriever and like a fisherman, he stuck the long pole out and set the small cage over the ball, turned it upside down and pulled the retriever to himself. In his hand was a Titleist Two—a ball that no doubt had only been hit once. It was perfect and would resell for at least $1.50. What a find, and it came right from the forbidden Triangle, the Bermuda Triangle of the Links. With that status, he'd ask his dad if he could charge $3.00 for it.

That evening, Lloyd took the ball to his room and set it on a shelf, right next to a foul ball his dad had caught off the bat of George Brett before Lloyd was born. He had kept it for the son he would have someday. Also on the shelf was a football signed by the Rose Bowl Champion Michigan Wolverines. And to show equal time, as he was too young to have any strong allegiance, he had a basketball signed by the MSU Spartan NCAA Basketball Champions of 2000.

Lloyd went to bed at his normal bedtime, which in the summer was after the sun had gone down. His mother turned the light off and kissed him good night. He lay there thinking about the day when it happened. A sound began. It was like a far away voice, but it wasn't a voice. It sounded scared or frightened perhaps, but you couldn't make out any words. Lloyd thought it was some kids outside as it was a warm, summer night. But, the more he listened, the more he knew the sound was in his room.

The sound stopped as Lloyd was going to leave his bed and tell his mom and dad. Just as the sound stopped, a picture fell from his wall and startled him. Then he saw the shadows on the wall. He couldn't make out what it was. He flew out of bed and ran to the door. He couldn't open it. The knob didn't budge. It was as if a strong force was keeping him in the room. He flicked up the light switch, but no light came on. He called out for his dad, but his dad didn't come.

Lloyd's breathing was fast and labored by now. He was truly frightened and began to panic. Finally, in what seemed an eternity, the door opened, and there stood his mother. She scooped him up in her arms and comforted him. He was panting, crying, and clinging to her.

"What's wrong, Tiger? What's the matter? Did you have a bad dream?"

"I heard sounds, then my picture fell, and then, I saw shadows. My light wouldn't go on. I couldn't open the door," Lloyd said, sobbing.

"I think you were having a bad dream, honey. See, the light works and the picture is up on your wall. I don't hear anything and I don't see any shadows."

"It was scary, Mom."

"Well, I'm sure it was. Mommy's had some nightmares and they seem real, but when you wake up you realize that it was only a dream and you feel better. Like now, don't you feel better to realize that it was all a dream?"

"Yeah, I guess so."

Right then, the ball started to roll on the shelf. It eventually fell down to the floor, bounced and rolled to Lloyd's feet.

"Whoops, your ball rolled off the shelf, honey."

"How did that happen?" Lloyd asked.

"Well, I don't really know. The house settles sometimes. That's probably what happened," she said. "OK, let's get you back in bed."

"Leave the door open and the light on, please, Mom?"

"Sure, if that will help."

Lloyd's mother picked up the ball and placed it on the shelf. She tucked Lloyd in, gave him a kiss on his forehead, and said, "Good night, honey."

Then, she said to be reassuring, "Call me if you see or hear anything, okay? I'll come as soon as you call."

For the next several minutes it was quiet and Lloyd soon fell asleep. Then the ball lifted off the shelf. The sounds and shadows returned as well. Lloyd missed his visitors, who had come to call for the second time.

Chapter Five
Saturday August 27, 2005

The next morning at breakfast, Cliff Hooker came downstairs to enjoy a bowl of corn flakes and some orange juice.

"Jane, I found my Titleist Two ball."

"Really? Where was it?"

"On the shelf."

"What shelf?"

"Not sure. I found it on a shelf last night."

"Clifford Hooker, don't do this to me. Did you go out last night and prowl around?"

"Don't be silly. You know I was in bed next to you."

"I know that you were till I got to sleep, but I don't know what you did or where you might have gone after I got to sleep."

"I sure didn't go prowling around in the neighborhood. If I had, you'd hear about it from all the busybodies who keep an eye on this place 24 hours a day."

"You've got a point there. So you found your ball on a shelf?"

"Yeah, I think I saw our grandson in Phoenix."

"Our grandson in Phoenix? How could that be, Cliff?"

"I mean, I had a dream about him I guess. He's got a George Brett baseball. Did you know that? Yeah, and a U of M football and an MSU basketball."

"Really, I never heard about that."

"Yeah, I saw them. That's where I got my ball."

"How do you know it was your ball?"

"Because it was a Titleist Two."

"Well, I hate to burst your bubble, but there are thousands and thousands of Titleist Twos."

"Not that tell me where they are. There is only one, this one."

"Clifford, stop it. You're talkin' crazy again. Drives me nuts! Now stop it!" Jane went out of the kitchen, screaming and holding her head as if she had a terrible headache.

Jane got to her bedroom and picked up the phone and called her daughter in Phoenix. "I know it is very early, honey. Sorry, but I've got to know, does Tommy have a George Brett baseball, a U of M football and an MSU basketball in his room or anywhere in your house?"

"Oh, no, he's a solid Arizona State fan. I'm very certain he has none of those items you mentioned, Mom."

Jane sat on the bed and sobbed. This was taking its toll and she'd be in a mental health ward in the near future. She couldn't keep her sanity day after day. It was all too much. All she wanted was her obnoxious 350 pound man back. Oh, what she'd give for the good old days.

✎

Brooke thought it best to go public. Once again with Larry's blessing she contacted the editor of the paper to secure his support. He assigned a reporter to the case and told Brooke, "We'll make this topic a priority in the foreseeable future. You can work with one of our investigative reporters, Jessica Pond."

Brooke met with Jessica. "I'd like a story about the Triangle and it needn't be a huge story, but enough to encourage people with any information or past experience to come forth and speak to me."

"I'll get right on it. It will appear in tomorrow's paper," Jessica said.

"That would be great. I'm bringing in Dr. Luciano DiNatale, a specialist from New Jersey and he'll arrive today. I'd like him to hear from anyone who wishes to come forth with information."

Jessica Pond turned to her laptop computer and began to type,

> Finally, some research! The Bermuda Triangle at Ghostly Links Country Club will be the subject of some serious investigation. A well-known private and local investigator, Brooke Parmore will donate her time to try and unravel the mystery that hovers over this golf course.
>
> Dr. Luciano DiNatale, director of the Center for Extracelestial Studies in New Jersey will arrive in town today to assist Miss Parmore. If anyone has any information to share, you may call 555-8525 and an appointment will be scheduled. The investigators have pledged that any contributor of information will remain anonymous and no information will be released without consent. They stressed that public support is very important to solve this mystery that has been the center of intrigue for golfers since the course opened six years ago.

Luciano DiNatale exited the elevator on the main floor of his hotel. He looked in the lobby and found Brooke sitting in a leather chair flipping through a magazine.

"Miss Parmore. It gives me great pleasure to be with you and to see you once again."

Brooke rose, and greeted Luciano, "Dr. DiNatale, welcome, welcome indeed. How was your trip?" Brooke asked.

"Uneventful except for monitoring the quickening of my heartbeat in anticipation of being with you."

"I think your quickened heartbeat was undoubtedly the result of turbulence. Do you talk in this charming way all the time?" Brooke asked, a bit embarrassed.

"When in the presence of intense beauty, yes."

Brooke didn't quite know how to respond to this charm.

She decided to change the subject. "Larry and I are looking forward to dinner this evening. We are hoping you enjoy the English Inn."

"I'm sure I will. Speaking of Mr. Ball, I thought he would be with you?"

"Larry has a member-guest league that needs his attention. He'll join us at the Inn. He's looking forward to meeting you."

"I must say, I am looking forward to meeting him as well. I'm eager to meet the man who has won your heart."

The two went to the English Inn; met Larry who was seated alone at the table reserved for three, and enjoyed a marvelous evening with wine and delicious food. Toward the end of the evening an intense discussion took place about the paranormal and how this mystery at Ghostly Links might be solved.

As the three were about to leave the inn, Luciano once again expressed his joy at being asked to assist Brooke and Larry in solving the mystery at Ghostly Links. The two confirmed plans to meet for breakfast followed by work on the case commencing at eight o'clock in the morning.

Brooke left the hotel believing that the next several days would be enjoyable. In fact, this case might prove to be the highlight of her investigative career.

Chapter Six

Sunday, August 28, 2005

The huge Sunday morning edition of the *Gazette* was tossed on the porches of the community. After reading the article about the Triangle, a few people wanted to talk to Brooke and Luciano. They called the number in the article and made appointments in the late morning and afternoon. Among them were Estelle Cartright, Jane Hooker and Bishop Walker.

Later that morning, Estelle Cartright walked into the conference room at the Ghostly Links Country Club. She was early for her appointment. Estelle was eager to tell her story to someone who would understand the strange happenings in the Cartright family.

"Good morning, Mrs. Cartright. I'm Brooke Parmore and this is Dr. DiNatale from New Jersey. Thank you for coming. What do you have to tell us?"

"First of all, thank you for looking into this strange phenomenon. I've been hoping someone would explain this mysterious place."

"You're welcome. The more we learn from folks like you, the better our chances to figure out what's going on. What do you have for us?" Brooke asked.

"My son has Down's Syndrome. We have been supportive of Special Olympics, thinking it would be wonderful for John. He liked to play golf, even as a young boy. He's 27 now, but as a young boy he always seemed to have a golf club in his hand and in spite of his challenges, he was pretty good at hitting the ball and sinking a few putts.

"One day, the golf coach, in trying to find a facility that would allow the Special Olympics athletes to play for free, asked Mr. Ball about using his course for a practice facility. Larry said, sure. So John and the others, along with their coach, practiced here and even played a few holes.

"I was there and sat in a lawn chair up near the clubhouse," Mrs. Cartright explained. "I watched John with pride and tried to be supportive, but I was also trying to be an out-of-the-way mom. I noticed on the first hole that John hit his second, or third shot into the Triangle. He can't read well enough to understand the warning sign, and his coach was helping others on the fairway. Anyway, John went into the Triangle and after a few minutes came back out. He kept on playing the hole and at least from where I was sitting, everything seemed normal."

"Did you get concerned?" Brooke asked.

"Yes. I, like most, know that the Triangle is a strange place. I was thankful John came out, and I just figured all was OK. I didn't want all the attention on him that resulted from the man who recently was in the news. John seemed fine so I relaxed a bit."

"I take it something did happen in the Triangle, Mrs. Cartright?" Luciano asked.

"Yes, it must have been the Triangle, because ever since then, John has no interest in golf. His only interest is astrophysics."

"Astrophysics?" Brooke asked, astounded at what she had heard.

"Yes. He spends hours at his computer, and in his spare time reads Hawking and Sagan. He's involved in a chat group discussing things about the universe that I don't understand. He might as well be talking Russian."

"Really. This is fascinating," Luciano said, taking notes.

"He has also befriended a scientist at NASA, who doesn't know he has Downs, by the way, and this scientist wants John to come to Houston for discussions and lectures and an interview for a possible place on a future space trip. I think it is for the first trip out of the Milky Way. Something that hasn't even been released to the media as yet."

"Sounds exciting," Luciano said, continuing to take notes.

"Yes, I guess it is. I pulled John from school and kept him home. We go to the stores and to movies and he gets out, but I can't have anybody finding out about this. I don't want him labeled again. A genius with Downs is unheard of. I mean, Downs is synonymous with retardation. Children and young adults with Downs are able to show the public far greater skills than decades ago, but retardation is still an aspect of the syndrome. So, if the world finds out about John's now being a genius, I don't think he, nor I, can handle what would happen to him. So, I hope God forgives me if I'm doing something wrong, but I simply can't let this out."

"We understand, Mrs. Cartright," Brooke said assuredly.

"I wouldn't be here except the article in the paper said that you would keep things from the media. I trust you to do this. You will keep this to yourselves, right?"

"Oh, most assuredly, Mrs. Cartright. You have our word," Brooke said while Luciano nodded his agreement with Brooke's pledge.

"So, no doctor knows of this change in John?" Brooke asked. "Nobody knows but you and the two of us, correct?"

"Yes, that's correct. I mean, many intellectuals know of him through the Internet, but they have no idea that he is Downs."

"Have you noticed anything strange?" Brooke asked.

"Stranger than what I just told you?"

"No, I mean, have you seen any ghosts, or heard strange sounds or seen things move or anything like that?"

"No, not really. Sometimes, I think I hear someone in John's room, but when I go in, it's just John. So, it's probably my imagination."

"John doesn't talk about anything strange, I take it?"

"The only thing that I can't understand is his priest friend."

"His priest friend?" Luciano asked.

"Yes. Recently he seems to either have an imaginary friend who is a priest or he's talking about someone in his chat group.

Who knows with John anymore, but yes, he sometimes talks about a priest friend. He says this priest tells jokes."

"Does he ever mention a name?" Luciano asked.

"No, not a name. He just calls him 'The Priest.'"

"OK."

"Is there anything else you would like to share with us?" Brooke asked.

"No, just my hope that you will keep all of this to yourselves."

"That's a given," Brooke replied.

🕊

Larry Ball knocked and opened the door to the conference room. "Sister is here."

"Sister? I don't have a sister, is your sister here, Luciano?"

"No, not your sister, a Sister, you know a Catholic nun."

"But, she doesn't have an appointment," Brooke said.

"OK, you tell her to go away then," Larry said.

"We can't be rude. Invite her in," Brooke replied.

An attractive, middle-aged nun came into the room. She stood before the two investigators seemingly in a world of confusion.

"Welcome, Sister," Brooke said. "Please sit down."

"I'm sorry I didn't make an appointment."

"You're forgiven—whoops, sorry, guess we're not in a position to be forgiving Sisters are we," Brooke said. All three smiled.

"I'll accept your forgiveness. Thank you," replied the nun.

"What do you have for us today?"

"My name is Sister Mulligan and I have come to see you. I read the article in the *Gazette* this morning. To put it as simply as I can, I have fear."

"Fear?"

"Yes, fear. A ghost has been present in the convent for the past few days. We don't know if it is related to this Triangle we've been reading about, but we thought it wouldn't do any harm to come in and tell you what we are experiencing."

Luciano was especially interested in Sister Mulligan's observations and led the questioning.

"Thanks so much for coming over, Sister. Please tell us what you see and what makes you so sure it's a ghost."

"We think we see a real person."

"A real person?"

"Well, yes. I mean it looks like a real person."

"It?"

"Yes, a ghost seems to be hanging out at the convent, but we can't be certain if it is a man or a woman. Some think it is Father Jim."

"Father Jim? What makes you think it might be him?"

"The jokes."

"Jokes?"

"Yes, we listen and we laugh and the only person we ever knew who told those kinds of nasty jokes was Father Jim."

"But you are not sure if the ghost is Father Jim?"

"Maybe it is and maybe it isn't."

"How do you mean? You said it was a real person in appearance. When you look at him, or it, you must either recognize him or not. I don't understand," Luciano said, confused.

"We don't know if it is Father Jim because facial features are unclear. When the Sisters talk about it, after it appears and tells jokes, some think the voice is Father Jim's because it sounds like a male voice, but others think not. They believe that the others are simply associating the jokes with the man and thinking it must be Father Jim."

"So, we have a ghost with no facial features, who tells jokes to the nuns?" Luciano asked.

"Yes."

"When do you see it?" Brooke asked.

"Usually just during recreation. The ghost is very respectful and doesn't seem to appear during prayers, Mass or study. We appreciate that," Sister Mulligan said, showing a beautiful smile.

"Anything else?"

"Well, the real reason I came here is to tell you that this ghost, if it is a ghost, tells us about a friend named Cliff."

"Really?" Brooke asked.

"Cliff who?" Luciano inquired.

"Well, I'm not one hundred percent certain but I think it

could be the Cliff on TV a while back who went into the Triangle and came out okay. Remember that?"

"Yes, I do. I'll explain further later, Luciano," Brooke said.

"Well, this ghost says that Cliff has seen the light, so to speak, and has converted to Catholicism. The ghost said that to celebrate the capturing of a soul, a crucifix was hung in Cliff's physical life home."

"Hmmm."

"I'm tempted to go to the Hooker home and talk to Cliff and invite him to church and to talk to Mrs. Hooker, but I can't find the courage to do this. It might be too upsetting to Mrs. Hooker."

"That was probably a wise decision, Sister," Brooke said.

"Have you two got any advice for us? I mean, we really don't mind the ghost, and the jokes are really quite humorous as long as we confess to hearing them and we ask forgiveness daily. But, I do know this, if the ghost is Father Jim and if he starts bringing this Cliff around, we're going to ask the Bishop to intervene. We simply can't be having these men traipsing all over the convent, who knows what they might see and do."

Luciano spoke up. "I think the only thing to do is to keep calm and to put up with the ghost and since none of you find it threatening, I guess, you could try to ignore it and eventually, it, like a physical soul, would decide to go elsewhere."

"Generally, I say that's good advice, but it's so hard to ignore Father Jim's jokes. I'll tell the Sisters to try and ignore him and to stifle any giggles. You know that laughing only reinforces him to keep coming back with more jokes.

"A priest would never tell these kinds of jokes to Sisters on the physical plane, so if it is Father Jim, he's getting away with something here. He is so sly, the jokes always occur when our Mother Superior is not present."

"Luciano and I could use some humor, perhaps you could ask the ghost to entertain us if he or she or it needs an audience," Brooke said.

Sister Mulligan left feeling better that others now knew of the jokester who, like a fall mist, comes and goes with lots of humorous stories echoing throughout the convent.

Chapter Seven

Brooke and Luciano went into town for some lunch. They needed to get away from the golf course for awhile. They had had an intense morning with much to think about.

In addition to people coming forward, the article touched off a wave of renewed interest in the Triangle. The community and others for miles beyond now focused attention on the triangular plot of land. The article caught the attention and interest of many newspaper editors across the country as the item came across the AP wire.

A local radio station got involved. They wanted to broadcast live from inside the Triangle if they could find any community celebrities to agree to be guests. *The Survivors* television show's producer called as they wanted to involve the Triangle for their contestants to try and win an immunity challenge.

Even though Jessica Pond's newspaper article stirred the community, Brooke and Luciano would be able to use all of the generated information to help solve the mystery.

❧

In the afternoon, Brooke and Luciano had appointments with Jane Hooker and Bishop Walker. Jane Hooker arrived and appeared quite nervous.

"Thank you for coming in to see us Mrs. Hooker," Brooke said.

"What information do you have to help us," Luciano asked.

"I hope you can solve this mystery. Nothing I say will leave this room. After all, that's what you both promised me for my information. Correct?"

"Absolutely, Mrs. Hooker," Brooke replied.

"There is much that I will not share with you, but this I will. Shortly after Cliff came out from the Triangle, he began to have more energy. Since that day he has been like a little kid who is hyperactive. I can't keep up with him. He exercises for hours at a time. He's lost almost a hundred pounds. Did either of you see the movie *Cocoon* several years ago?" Brooke and Luciano nodded affirmatively.

"Well, that is how Cliff is, only much more youthful and on the go all the time."

"In a sense, that is good, isn't it, Mrs. Hooker?" Brooke asked.

"Good, if I had a Harley to keep up with him, yeah. But my concern, and the reason I'm here to talk to you, is that what happened in the Triangle is what gives him this energy. I'll tell you this; the Fountain of Youth is right outside your door. That Triangle is Ponce De Leon's dream come true.

"If I were the owner of this place, I'd sell tickets for the chance to go in there for 10,000 dollars a minute and I'd have more customers than I'd ever have room for in that Triangle of land. I say this assuming it will make people happy. For me, it has done just the opposite and I can't speak for Cliff."

"Anything else to share?" Luciano asked.

"Yes. The thing that has me really upset is that Cliff wants to join the Catholic Church."

"What is he now?" Brooke asked.

"We are Jehovah's Witnesses. This Catholic stuff is all because of that Triangle. Not only have I lost my fat and obnoxious husband of many years, but I am now denied eternal life with my Cliff. He's gone Catholic and he's got a crucifix on the living room wall. All he talks about is going to Mass. He watches Sister Angelica on the Catholic cable channel. It's ridiculous."

"I'll bet that's hard to accept," Luciano said in sympathy.

"Hard to accept? It's the difference between heaven and hell and we're talking for all of eternity. And, that's not all. Cliff has begun to tell the most awful jokes about the clergy. The jokes are terrible and offensive and so unlike Cliff. I mean, he'd tell an occasional off-color joke, but he never used to tell these low-life stories and stories one would never tell a woman, and especially a woman who is a Jehovah's Witness."

Brooke and Luciano looked at each other. Their eyes connected and for the first time they really did see a link. Without talking they fully believed that not only did these people come back to the earth as ghosts, but that they lived a dual existence. They were real people when they wanted to be people and ghosts when they wanted to be ghosts.

Mrs. Hooker went on for several more minutes. Before leaving she announced that the result of Cliff walking into the Triangle has stressed her marriage to the point of possibly seeking a divorce. She couldn't keep on living in this crazy relationship and maintain her sanity.

≈

Bishop Walker was next. He came in alone and sat down. He refused any coffee or water. He looked pale and tired.

"Are you feeling OK?" Brooke asked.

"I think so. It's been a crazy week."

"I'm sorry, but I think we both understand."

"Thank you. I hope you won't tell anyone as I sure don't want this to get out, but I think I'm seeing ghosts."

"Is it Father Jim?" Brooke inquired.

"No, should it be?" the Bishop asked.

"I guess not, just thought that is what you would tell us," Brooke replied.

"No, Father Jim came to my office after that Triangle experience. We had a good talk and I thought he needed a break. That guy's been under a lot of stress himself. I sent him to a retreat house in Connecticut for a month or so. Hopefully, he will come back refreshed and ready to tackle all the needs of his parishioners."

"Could you give us the name of the retreat house?" Luciano asked.

"Sure. It's St. Dominic's, outside of Hartford. It's a popular place."

"Please, tell us more about this ghost," Brooke said.

"Well, the only place I see it is at the 6 a.m. Mass. Not many people come to this first Mass of the day, but those who come are regulars. Anyway, I digress a bit. I go through my usual routine and then just as the Mass is about to start, a door opens in the back of the church and then closes with no one present. I'm the only one who sees this as all others are facing me.

"This ghost, or at least I call it a ghost, sits in the back which I appreciate by the way. I suppose if he or she or it came down to the front, others might see this spirit as well, and man oh man, would I have some explaining to do. Actually, I do have some explaining to do because the people see me hold up the host and say, 'The body of Christ' and then it disappears like magic. I've heard that some of the regulars call me Father Magic and some are beginning to invite friends to see this 'trick' as they call it. One of my more charismatic parishioners has just begun to spread a rumor that this is a saint who appears each morning. One of my parishioners is proclaiming that the Virgin Mary comes each day to receive her Son back from the cross. It doesn't take much to get some of my people going, especially those with a vivid imagination."

"CBS News will be doing a documentary pretty soon," Luciano predicted.

"Well, my dilemma is this. I think I know the ghost and I know the ghost is a Catholic soul and I can't refuse Christ to him. I have my vows to consider as well. So, my dilemma is conducting the Mass appropriately, and on the other hand, inviting a side show of enormous proportions."

"Who do you think is the ghost?" Brooke asked.

"Father Jim introduced him to me when I invited Jim to get some rest at St. Dominic's. I really can't recall his name right off, but I'd certainly recognize him. He's a big man."

"How can you be sure he is a Catholic?"

"Father Jim told me he was."

"What would you say if I told you that ghost was not a Catholic but a Jehovah's Witness?"

Bishop Walker sat back and gave a hearty laugh. "Oh, that is a good one, Miss Parmore. That would be hilarious."

"Well, that's what I think is happening."

"How so?"

"Do you know Cliff Hooker, the golfer who went into the Triangle and was also on TV?" Brooke asked.

"I don't know him, but yes, I heard about him."

"I think the ghost is Cliff Hooker."

"But he isn't dead. He's alive, living with his wife, Jane. I think that's her name, from what I read in the paper. You can't be a ghost unless you're dead."

"Well, maybe that's the way it used to be."

"Used to be?"

"Maybe we all have the power to be on more than one level of existence at the same time and some of us choose to live that way, I mean to express the spirit plane on the physical plane."

"That's an interesting thought. So, let me try to understand. You are saying you think Cliff Hooker, the Jehovah's Witness on the physical plane, is also Cliff Hooker, the Catholic, on the ethereal plane, and that the two are the same?"

"Well, the same energy, yes," Brooke said.

"An interesting thought. A very interesting thought. But, why don't we see those ghosts all the time?"

"Choice."

"Choice?"

"The energies choose where to be and when and maybe there are more than two planes, but two is all our senses are capable of comprehending and most people refuse to admit to the existence of a spirit plane, as you know.

"Do you mind if we call St. Dominic's and would you talk to the director and ask about Father Jim?" Brooke asked. "I'll bet if he is honest, we'll learn that strange things are going on in the state of Connecticut."

"Fine with me. I have the number here in my planner."

The call was placed. "Hello, this is Bishop Walker calling to see how Jim McDuffy is doing?"

"He's resting. But, I'm glad you called because since Jim's been here, we've been having some strange things happen."

"Strange, in what way?" Bishop Walker asked.

"Our Brothers claim to be hearing things, seeing things, just spooky stuff."

"Probably just their imagination."

"Yeah, but Father Jim seems to disappear and then later will reappear."

"Maybe you should record what happens."

"OK, but I'll be happy when you call Father McDuffy home. All was relatively normal until he arrived. And, his jokes, Bishop. They are so bad. Can't you do something to discipline this man?"

"I've tried. Lord knows, I've tried. I'll talk to him."

"Thanks."

Bishop Walker told Brooke and Luciano what he had learned. The investigators noted the information while Bishop Walker sat stunned.

Chapter Eight

Brooke asked Larry if they could talk to some members of the grounds department, particularly anyone who wanted to share information about the Triangle. A meeting was set up for late in the afternoon. Only two men volunteered to share their experiences. They were Rick Clubb and Sam Player. Their clothes were dirty from a day's work and their hands were greasy. Both removed their caps as they entered the room.

Brooke welcomed them. "Thank you for coming. This is Dr. Luciano DiNatale from New Jersey. We're looking into the mystery of Ghostly Links. The reason for the meeting is to listen to you, and see if you have had any experiences, or thoughts you'd like to share."

"I guess I could begin. My name is Rick Clubb. I've got a story for you."

"Thank you, Rick. Tell us what you do at Ghostly Links," Brooke said.

"I do general maintenance. What I want to share happened a few years ago, when I was mostly responsible for smoothing the traps on the course."

"OK, tell us what happened," Brooke said.

"Well, early one morning, before players were allowed on the course, I went to the 14th hole, and I don't know if you folks have been all over the course, but there is a huge trap to the right of the green. It takes me at least a half hour to smooth that trap.

"I went there one morning to begin my work. Right in the middle of the trap was one of them sand castles you see at the beach. It was quite a thing of beauty, actually. I hated to knock it down, but it was my job to smooth the traps."

"The castle was the work of some high school kids looking for fun on a summer night, Rick. How many times do I have to tell you that?" Sam Player said, shaking his head and making fun of his co-worker.

"That's what you've always said. But there were no footprints around that castle. No footprints in the grass either. There is no way a human being could have done that."

"Did it ever occur to you that the kids used the rake to smooth out the trap when they were finished? Come on, Rick. Pay the rent on your upstairs!"

"There was no rake at the trap," Rick snapped back.

"Then they brought their own," Sam argued.

"The rake I used had a missing tooth second from the end and all through the trap was evidence of the tooth being missing. The trap was just as I left it except in the middle was this huge and beautiful sand castle."

"Did you take a photo of it, Rick?" Luciano asked.

"Of course he didn't," Sam replied. "How can you take a photo of something that doesn't exist? If my theory is wrong that kids were looking for something to do, then Rick made the whole thing up. I will say this for Rick. He does have a vivid imagination."

Rick muttered some obscenity under his breath and fired it toward Sam. Brooke thought that it would have been better to have talked individually with each worker, but it was too late.

"Listen, you folks don't have to believe me. I came here to tell you I seen a sand castle in the trap on 14 and I don't need this guy hassling me. I'm out of here." Rick stood up and headed toward the door.

"Thank you, Mr. Clubb. We may be contacting you," Luciano said.

"Fine, but don't bring Player with you! I'm going to the bar; I need a drink and friends."

Sam shook his head. "Guy's crazy. I'm sorry, I guess I got a bit carried away, but if you had to work with Rick, you'd go nuts in a week. He's got weird things going on all around him. Makes it all up to get sympathy or attention. I just don't like him, is all."

"What did you come here to tell us, Sam?" Brooke asked.

"Well, for what it's worth, I want to say that, I think, this is all a bunch of baloney. I'm convinced that all of this is simply an excellent example of the mind playing tricks based on suggestions. All you need to do is think you'll see a ghost and one pops up. People love to talk about all of this. It makes for interesting conversation.

"You'd think there was enough crazy, legitimate stuff going on in the world to talk about without living in a fantasy world about all of these ghosts."

"So, this is all in people's imaginations?" Brooke asked.

"As far as I'm concerned it is."

"What do you do out here, Sam?" Luciano asked.

"Like Rick, I'm maintenance. I do grass cutting, green cutting, odd jobs, tree trimming, cup changes. I've worked here since the course opened. The superintendent has given me just about all the jobs possible at one time or another."

"Thanks. What more can you tell us?"

"The ghosts people claim to see are nothing more than fog. The land in that patch of ground they call the Triangle is warmer than the surrounding air and when people say they see a mist, they're right; they see a mist, but not a ghost."

"Ever read that book in the clubhouse with the strange happenings out here?" Sam asked. Brooke nodded, but Luciano admitted not knowing of the book.

"Well, that's one storyteller trying to outdo the next. None of that stuff happened. Old men just like to read that kind of stuff. Every golfer misses a putt or two per round, each one thinks it was heading for the cup and can't understand why the ball didn't go in the hole. Well, the ball didn't go in the hole because the green's surface has a small indentation near the cup, it is all explainable.

"The mind is very powerful. Once something is suggested, it is in the brain and sure enough, you begin to see what you hear about. It's like this. If you buy a Volkswagen Beetle, for example, and take it for a drive, then you begin to see all kinds of Volkswagens. They're everywhere and you never noticed them before. The same thing is at work out here. You call a golf course the Ghostly Links, you have a Spooktacular Outing, you tell people to sign a release slip because strange things happen in a triangle of land and sure enough, people start seeing things, hearing things, and having crazy experiences. If you call the course Tall Pines, you see tall pines, call it Rolling Meadows and you see rolling meadows, and you call it Ghostly Links and you see Ghosts. It don't take a rocket scientist to figure this out."

"You've got a good point there," Luciano said, impressed with Sam's explanations.

"Have you ever gone into the Triangle, Sam?" Brooke asked.

"Yeah, I walked in once, just to prove that everyone was crazy thinking things happen to people."

"What did you see?" Luciano asked.

"Nothing."

"Nothing? No golf balls?"

"Nothing. Just a rough with lots of brush, trees, and long grass."

"Did anything change in your life after you went into the Triangle, Sam?" Luciano asked.

"Change?"

"Yeah, I mean, could you do something you couldn't do before you went in? Did you have a wish come true for example?"

"Wife left me, if you can call that a wish come true."

"I suppose it could be, if you didn't love her or want her around," Luciano reasoned.

"I made a mistake. Married young, immature, her escape from an abusive home. But her leaving had nothing to do with my walking into that Triangle, I know that. Listen, divorces happen every day, thousands of them and people don't go walking around in the rough of golf courses before signing the papers."

"That's true," Brooke admitted.

"How's your health?" Luciano asked.

"Good, now."

"Now? It hasn't always been good?"

"Yeah, pretty good. I had a sore back from a football injury, but lately, it's been OK."

"Did it get better after you went into the Triangle?"

"Well, yeah, since then, I guess, but I didn't walk out with a pain-free back, if that's what you mean."

"I'm just looking for anything that may have changed in your life after you were in the Triangle."

"Once again, look for something and you'll find it. Bound to happen."

"Anything else to share?" Brooke asked.

"Nah, I've got to go and buy Rick a beer or two. That usually patches things up when I say something stupid."

"Thanks for coming in," Luciano said. "We appreciate it."

✺

Luciano's cell phone rang. He took it from his belt and answered.

"Is this Dr. DiNatale?"

"Yes."

"Thank goodness. I'm happy to reach you."

"How can I help you?"

"I am Doctor Trevino in Lubbock, Texas. I have a patient who's quite distraught. She thinks she has come under the influence of a ghost. I went to the Internet and your name comes up frequently and so I thought you might be of some help."

"I'll try," Luciano offered. "I'm involved in a case in the Midwest at the moment. But, let me try and answer any questions you have, and then if I am still needed, perhaps I can be of assistance once my work is finished here."

"Thank you. My patient is a pro golfer in the LPGA. As best as I can tell she seems to think she has a second caddy. She sees some ghost-like figure sometimes, but not always. Her caddy smokes and so she thinks what she sees is smoke patterns from the caddy but maybe it's some ghostly form. What is obvious is advice, unsolicited advice."

"Advice?" Luciano asked.

"Yeah, what club to use, the distance to the pin, something to consider before hitting the shot."

"Hmmm, she's not sure the voice is her own, sort of talking to herself?" Luciano asked, looking for an explanation.

"I asked that, and no, the voice, if we can call it that, is not hers. By the way, she says that the advice is usually very helpful. She's not complaining. She merely wants me to assure her that she's normal.

"I'm trying to do that, but I thought I'd check with an expert to see if there is any literature about athletes being banned because they think they are being advised by a ghost or spirit in some form. I think she fears that if this becomes known she'd be considered a nut, ostracized by those on the tour."

"A ghostly advisor. Boy, don't we all wish we had one and especially if the advice is helpful!" Luciano said, making light of the information he had just been given.

"Yeah, I know what you mean."

"Well, the answer to your question is, no. I've known popular personalities having encounters with spirits, but to repeat, not an athlete getting advice while in competition."

"Any advice to help my client?" Dr. Trevino asked.

"I'd sure like to talk to this golfer and learn more," Luciano said.

"I'll ask her if she'd be willing to share the information with you and if she consents, I'll ask her to call."

"Thank you."

"Thank you, Dr. DiNatale. You've been most helpful."

Luciano set his cell phone on the table.

"Who was that if I may ask?" Brooke said.

"A psychiatrist in Texas who has a patient who is playing on the women's professional tour who thinks she hears a ghost giving her advice."

"Probably Carolyn Spiker."

"Carolyn?"

"Yes, the golfer who went into the Triangle looking for Father Jim and Reverend Hogan. She came out, but this is the first time any reference to her has appeared."

"What am I missing?" Luciano said looking a bit confused. "I don't see any connection."

"Golf."

"Golf?"

"Yeah, she was a good golfer," Brooke recalled. "In the spirit life, I'm sure she would love to be on a golf course, and if she can't play in a physical sense, at least she can play through others and if she has any advice for the golfer on the physical plane, why not share it? So, she does."

"This is a professional golfer, Brooke."

"All the more reason to know that it is Carolyn. How much more glamorous can it get? Crowds, excitement, tension, and competition makes her job as an Episcopal priest pale by comparison."

❧

The two investigators discussed what they had heard throughout the day. Brooke found it all fascinating, but for Luciano it was just another day at the shop. He'd heard so many stories of ghosts and strange phenomenon that today's stories were nothing more than another group of people finding themselves in a strange environment, an environment that Luciano came to accept as quite normal.

"I'm curious about the line," Brooke said, appearing to be deep in thought.

"The line? What line?"

"The line between the rough and the Triangle. I mean there has to be some demarcation point when the human enters the Triangle and crosses some imaginary line."

"Well, yes. In our physical world of unbounded energy we do have separated fields and you're curious if a sort of imaginary rope encircles this land."

"Yeah, I mean, does the force at work here extend out and affect people in the rough just a little bit or must the human literally step over a line, you know, like the characters in *Field of Dreams*."

"Characters in *Field of Dreams?*" Luciano asked, confused.

"You know the movie, where the doc stops short of stepping over the baseline to help the choking girl, or where the James Earl Jones' character stops and laughs before going into the corn field."

"Oh, yes. Well, my thinking is that, as you put it, there's a definite demarcation point from non-Triangle to Triangle. You're either in it, or not, and my guess is that it happens as soon as the person steps from the rough into the Triangle proper, and for me, that means taller grass."

"Yes, but it's not often a clear boundary," Brooke said.

"I agree, but one knows if he's in the rough or in the Triangle and I think that's the factor," Luciano replied.

"Could someone reach in so that their hand is in the Triangle but the rest of their body is not and have something happen or must the whole body be in the Triangle?" Brooke asked, full of curiosity.

"My guess would be that the space is the force as opposed to the surface."

"I mean, tens of golfers must have come up to the Triangle and while going in would have reached past this line of demarcation with a club to move some of the grass and shrub trying to see if their ball was on the edge. If they see it, they undoubtedly draw it out with the club head. I wonder if anything ever happened to these people?"

"My guess is that whatever energy is focused in the Triangle affects anyone, even if, as you say, the person reaches into the undefined boundary," Luciano said, realizing that someone may not need to walk into the Triangle proper to encounter the energy.

Chapter Nine

Lucy Putterbee was an avid golfer who took up golf following a traumatic divorce. She liked getting her mind on a white ball and the beautiful surroundings of nature and off of her personal crisis. She took a few lessons from Larry and then with a lot of play, found herself becoming quite good. In fact, if anyone has a chance to beat Jane Hooker, it would be Lucy Putterbee.

Lucy had had an experience with the Triangle but didn't want to share it with Brooke and Luciano. One day, Lucy hit a shot that went into the Triangle. It had been quite dry for several days and the ball rolled and skipped along toward the Triangle. Lucy thought she could find it and indeed she did. She could see it about a foot into the Triangle.

Lucy took warning signs seriously and would never consider stepping foot into the mythical abyss. But, there was her ball and so she thought there would be no harm in reaching in and taking it, so she did. She felt nothing out of the ordinary. As far as Lucy could tell, she didn't have any physical reaction to her bold move. She breathed a sigh of relief and then hit her third shot taking a penalty shot for the unplayable lie. Lucy completed her round with a good score for her, but nothing to set the world on fire.

Lucy's son Rick, age 15, wanted to learn how to play the piano, so Lucy dipped into her savings and arranged for Rick to take lessons. She couldn't afford a piano, but she could afford an electronic keyboard and with advice from Rick's teacher she purchased one. Rick didn't have any natural talent, but liked the sound and unlike most kids his age, he did practice. He had the maturity to know the sacrifice that his mom was making in allowing him to have some lessons and to buy a keyboard.

After dinner on the day Lucy reached into the Triangle to get her ball, Rick asked Lucy a question, "Mom, what key do I play in if I have one sharp?"

"I don't know. I don't know anything about music. Ask your teacher, or look it up someplace. It's probably in one of your music books."

"Mom, does this chord sound right? Am I playing the right notes?"

Again Lucy responded, "I don't know, honey. I have no ear for that kind of thing. I want to help you, but I don't know one key from another."

Rick continued to practice and Lucy was proud that he took the hobby seriously, which justified her financial sacrifice.

After dinner, Rick went outside to play baseball with friends. Lucy found herself drawn to the keyboard. She touched a few notes and found that they sounded like a familiar tune. So, she experimented and within seconds, with only her right hand, she was using chords and playing notes that errorlessly and easily filled the room with familiar tunes.

Lucy brought her left hand up to the keyboard, but nothing happened. The fingers didn't seem to know where to go or what to do, while the right hand seemed to be on automatic pilot, playing songs from her childhood.

Lucy was shocked. She had not taken piano lessons as a child. The only way to explain what was happening, Lucy reasoned, was to believe that she had inherited the "gift" as her mother always used to call it when she came upon someone who could play by ear. However, upon reflection, she did remember banging around on a friend's piano as a child, trying to play "Happy Birthday" or "Auld Lang Syne," but none of the notes seemed to be right. She abandoned any further efforts after sensing frustration.

Then, it hit her like a bolt of lightning; the hand she could now play the piano with was the hand she used to retrieve the ball earlier in the day at Ghostly Links. The obvious question she asked herself was, what would happen if I reached into the Triangle to get a ball with my left hand?

The next day she played golf at Ghostly Links. When she arrived at the Triangle, she went to the same spot, took a ball and from about 10 feet out rolled the ball into the Triangle. She then stepped up and with her left hand reached in and took the ball. So curious was she that she did not complete her round. She went directly home and sat at the keyboard. With her right hand she began to play a favorite song. She then raised her left hand to the keyboard and as if the appendage knew exactly what to do, it began to play chords to correspond perfectly to the melody being played in the treble clef.

"Oh, my God!" she exclaimed. "This is a miracle!" She spent the next hour gleefully playing most of her favorite songs and thoroughly enjoying the experience.

Once she left the keyboard, she was faced with how to tell people about what had happened. Should she contact the media with her story? Should she make up a phony explanation? Or, should she just accept what happened and keep it a secret from everyone, including Rick?

Lucy decided to explain it in this way: she'd tell people that she got one of those "Anyone Can Learn to Play the Piano" videotapes in the mail. The instructions plus some innate talent, brought this out. Who could doubt that? She didn't want to go to the media lest thousands go to the Triangle thinking they would be instant pianists. Maybe they would, but Lucy didn't want this circus atmosphere because of her story.

She would play for friends and family and found that in addition to golf, playing the piano was great fun and a marvelous new avocation.

If anyone asked her to play she decided she would break into "Hokey-Pokey" and smile as people sang, "You put your right hand in, you put your right hand out, you put your right hand in and you shake it all about." Lucy thought. *If these people only knew*!

Lucy thought about putting her right and left foot into the Triangle, wondering if she would become a ballerina or if she could dance like Ginger Rogers, but she didn't tempt fate. She would never know what would happen because she decided to let well enough alone and simply be thankful for discovering a new talent.

✐

Lucy had to tell somebody about this miracle. She knew that she could trust her good friend, Ella Sorenstam, who had been a friend since they were schoolgirls twenty-some years ago. She knew that Ella could keep a secret so she asked her to come over for a cup of coffee.

What Lucy didn't realize was that Rick was within earshot when they sat down to share Lucy's amazing story. Rick saw his mother's obvious joy and the simplicity with which the "gift" had come to her.

The next day, Rick went to the Ghostly Links. He knew Larry the pro and said he wanted to go out on the course looking for golf balls. Larry knew that Rick and his mom had limited resources, so if finding and selling a few balls would help out the Putterbees, he wanted to be supportive.

"Sure, Rick. Hope you find some good ones. Stay away from the Triangle, now, ya hear?"

"Oh, yeah. I know that's off limits, but I'll bet that Triangle has a million balls in it, don't you think so, Mr. Ball?"

"Yeah, someday a volcano might rise up and we'll have millions of golf balls all over the place." The two chuckled.

"Say, Rick. Did you make the baseball team this year? I know you're a pretty good pitcher."

"Tryouts are tomorrow. I'm not doing very good. The fast ball isn't fast enough, my curve doesn't break, and my slider slides right onto the heart of the guy's bat."

"Ouch, that's not good news."

"Nope. I'll try out, but I don't expect to make the team. I was pretty good in junior high, but in high school, I'm just an also ran."

"Hey, chin up, young man," Larry said. "Do your best tomorrow. You'll do OK."

"Thanks."

Rick walked out the door and headed down the rough of the ninth fairway. He got to the sharp 45 degree corner of the Triangle, where the 8th green and 9th tee share about an acre.

Rick looked around as if he were about to take a chocolate chip cookie from the cookie jar and needed to be assured that Mom wasn't looking or that a sister or brother wouldn't see it and tell on him. He didn't see anybody.

As he approached the Triangle to put his hands in, he tripped on a gopher hole and fell forward into the Triangle. He quickly got up and brushed the dirt off of his pants. He was only in the Triangle for a few seconds. To be sure his hands had been in the space; he stood on the edge and reached in as if one would reach out the door to see if it was raining.

He had completed his mission. Then he walked out to the woods by the fourth, fifth, and sixth holes where he found a dozen balls. On his way home, he stopped in at the pro shop to let Larry know that his trip was successful and to thank him for letting him go onto the course.

"Anytime, Rick. Thanks for checking in with me first."

"Sure."

"Say, Rick, did you hurt yourself with that fall?"

"Fall?"

"Tom Green said he saw you over by the Triangle. He said it looked like you tripped and fell."

"Yeah, I did, but I'm OK. I guess I stepped into a gopher hole. I didn't go into the Triangle, Mr. Ball."

"Oh, I know that, Rick. Tom just said you took quite a tumble out by the 9th tee and he hoped you were OK."

"Yeah, I'm OK."

Rick went home and immediately went to the keyboard. He took out some sheet music that he used for his lesson. He put both hands up to the keyboard expecting to be able to play Rachmaninoff, but nothing happened. He had no more talent than he did when he left for the course an hour ago.

Chapter Ten

Monday, August 29, 2005

Larry Ball was beginning to curse the day Jessica Pond's newspaper article appeared in the *Gazette*. He was sure that Brooke and Luciano were getting good information, but the article did what was not expected and that was to bring hundreds, and perhaps in the future, thousands of people to his course. There were traffic problems; the members couldn't get parking places. It was becoming a big problem.

Larry had a meeting with the city planner to see how this could be addressed. Ghostly Links was private property and citizens could not just wander onto it, but they did. He would get calls from physically disabled people who wanted to see if they could be healed. He got calls from tour directors who wanted to stop on the way to casinos so patrons could see the famous Bermuda Triangle of the Links.

Finally, Larry Ball sought out a marketing professor at the local university. The two had coffee. Larry said flat out, "I think I'm sittin' on a gold mine. I've got an attraction that could bring in millions of dollars, but I don't know how to pull it off, and still manage one of the finest golf courses in the world.

"I'm told that people throw money into the Triangle for good luck. Some treat it like a fountain and give it three coins.

I have golfers tell me as they walk along the fairway on 1, 8 or 9 that they'll heave a quarter or more into the Triangle to appease the golf gods. Really. I'm not making this up. I've got people throwing money at me, well not me, but at my course.

"I've got thousands of dollars of golf balls in the Triangle; I've got a pilgrimage site with caravans of people wanting to see it, hear about it, and I've got a lot of nuts at the university who want to run through it naked on a dare. I've even seen T-shirts on campus that say, '"Naked Co-Ed Triangle Run - 2005,'" Larry said, shaking his head in astonishment.

"I've hired nighttime security so nothing like this ever happens, but my point is, this is getting almost too much for me to handle and I'm wondering if I can turn a frustrating problem into a financial windfall. I want my members to play great golf, but inside of their course is this spectacle that thousands and perhaps millions want to see.

"This morning, I got a call from a movie producer. He's got big bucks and wants a movie shot here—thinks it could be an Academy Award winner. He says people love this kind of thing. I think he's the same guy who made *The Sixth Sense*, but I'm not sure.

"Finally, and then I'll be quiet and listen, I got an e-mail from a staff member for some famous writer, forget his name now, but this guy was doing some legwork for a novel.

"It doesn't stop. Oh, yes, a charity wants to have a run out here called, The Ghostly Links 10K—not very original, but it is one more example of people becoming fascinated with this thing and flocking to it.

"Well, I've gone on and on and not given you a chance to comment. So, I'll be quiet and listen to what you have to say," Larry said, leaning back in his chair with his fingers interlocked behind his head.

"I'll be short and to the point. You are sitting on millions of dollars. Managed well, you won Powerball at an all-time high! Congratulations. I don't know what you did to deserve this, but yes, you have Fort Knox right here at Ghostly Links."

"Hmmm, guess I just had the expert on *The Antiques Roadshow* tell me I was the owner of some rare piece of art."

"Well, yes, but it is worth, over time, billions."

"Billions? You really think so? What do I do?" Larry asked.

"You need a plan, and trust me, you can afford the finest minds in getting some help organizing and drawing from the public's fascination with this phenomenon while still allowing the golf course to maintain its prestige."

"I need to hire a public relations specialist to answer the phone and handle correspondence. If I don't do something pretty quick, this whole phenomenon will be out of control."

"Give Clarence Shank a call. His number is 555-7009. You don't need me anymore. Old Shank will take it from here. I'll just watch this financial empire grow and grow and be proud that I had a hand in getting you off to a good start."

*Brooke and Luciano wanted to talk to Cliff Hooker. Brooke called Jane and asked if they could talk to him. There was quite a period of silence and then Jane came back on, "Cliff and I will come over."

A half hour later, Cliff and Jane Hooker were sitting in the conference room of Ghostly Links. Brooke welcomed them and led the questioning.

"Cliff, we're hoping you can help us solve this mystery. We'd like to ask some questions. Is that all right with you?"

"Yeah, sure."

"Cliff, when you went into the Triangle, did you have any sensations?"

"Sensations?"

"Yes, did you feel any energy? Was it warm or cold? Did you hear any sounds?"

"Oh, I see. No, I was just looking for my golf ball. It didn't seem any different from any other walk in the woods looking for a ball, and I'm here to tell you, that in my fifty-odd years on the links, I've spent more time in the woods looking for my golf balls, than I have in the fairway. Right, Jane? You know that don't you, honey buns?" Cliff asked, and Jane smiled.

"Yes, Cliff is pretty wild on the golf course. I never get him any new golf balls for Christmas because he's collected so many traipsing through the woods looking for his prize Titleist Twos."

"I understand, Cliff. I've spent my share of time off the fairway as well," Luciano added.

"OK, you didn't have any sensations. Did you see anything out of the ordinary?" Brooke asked.

"Nope. Trees, thick brush, grass, fallen limbs, some marshy area and then a cave. I mean, it looked like a cave, an opening, pretty good size."

"An opening, huh?" Luciano asked.

"Yeah, looked like an opening to a cave."

"Big enough for a person to walk into?" Brooke asked.

"Yeah, for sure. Well, they'd have to stoop a bit. I'd say it was 5 feet high, maybe."

"But, you didn't walk into it?" Brooke asked.

"No."

"Did you see anybody, Cliff?"

"Nope."

"So, you simply walked into the woods, in this thick brush, looking for your ball. You found it and came out?" Brooke asked.

"Yes. But, I didn't find my ball. I mean, I found it later, but not in the woods."

"You didn't find it? You found another ball? There must be thousands in there."

"Yeah, I would think so, but now that you mention it, I didn't see any balls. I saw the ball I thought was mine, picked it up and then walked out to meet Jane."

"You said that you found your ball later, did you go back in?"

Jane interjected, "Cliff. That's enough, you've told them enough. I don't think it wise to go any further with this."

"The wife thinks I shouldn't talk about this, I guess."

"Hmm, just asking about your ball, the Titleist Two that you found later."

"I found it in a little boy's bedroom. I thought I was in Phoenix but I guess I wasn't."

"Cliff, I said that's enough! It's time to go."

"Mrs. Hooker, Cliff's information is very helpful to us and if we can learn what happens to those who have gone in, it might help a lot of people. We really need Cliff to tell us what he knows. Please? I assure you what Cliff tells us won't leave this room."

"I think it's okay to tell them, Sugar. What's the harm?"

"The harm is that it will leak and you'll be a freak."

"Hey, good line there. You're a poet and didn't know it, huh, Jane?"

"Please, Cliff, tell us about the Titleist Two," Brooke pleaded.

"I'm going to do it, Jane. I trust these people. We've got to help others." Jane shook her head in disagreement and disappointment, but Cliff had always been his own man.

"Well, my ball communicates with me."

Luciano sat up and took notice. He took over the questioning.

"Your ball talked to you?"

"Well, yes, but not in English like we talk. There seems to be an attraction frequency. That's the best way to describe it, I guess. The frequencies attract, yeah, that's it. I sort of feel like a radio station getting frequencies and I know where, in this case, the ball is, and I'm drawn to it."

"Does this work with people, too?"

"When my friend, who is known as Father Jim here on the physical plane, wants to tell me a joke or talk about things in our church, we communicate with these frequencies."

"That church is NOT your church, Cliff Hooker. Stop talking like that!"

"This gets Jane upset a bit. I'm a Jehovah's Witness here on the physical plane, but my spirit is Catholic."

"It is not, Cliff! We are in all ways Jehovah's Witnesses and will go to Heaven as such."

"There's no Heaven, Janie! Let me finish with these people."

"Whoa, slow down. No Heaven?" Brooke asked.

"Well, the highest frequency is Heaven, but it's no place, you know like a place with pearly gates and such. It's simply a collection of the highest frequencies, that's all. I don't think you folks can get it and I don't have any words to make it clear, I'm sorry."

"But you were saying about communicating with your friend," Luciano said, wanting to get the conversation back to Father Jim.

"Oh, yes, well it's frequency communication is all. That comes closest for you folks to understand what I'm trying to say."

"Do you see Father Jim?" Brooke asked.

"If I want to."

"What do you mean?"

"I can see him like you see him or I can see him as an energy field."

"Really?" Brooke asked intrigued by what she had heard.

"Yeah, but I can do the same with each of you right now. I can see your energy field and I can see you as a human form."

"Can you 'see' people who have died?"

"Oh sure. It's a marvelous reunion. You see, on the physical plane, all you think you can see or hear is what you get from your senses, which by the way isn't much as you'll see when you, as you call it, die."

"So, we don't die?" Brooke asked.

"Well, you die in a sense that your body doesn't function on the physical plane, but that's all."

"Is there a Hell?" Brooke asked.

"Hell, no," Cliff bellowed. "Gotcha! It's just low frequencies, the opposite of Heaven. What you call 'Heaven' is really high frequency and what you call 'Hell' is low frequency."

"Low frequency?"

"Well, once again, words can't do it. There's no harmony, no love energy. I don't know. You just need to experience it."

"Yeah, but I'm enjoying this plane at the moment," Brooke said with a smile.

"Illusion. You're already on the spiritual plane, which is THE plane, but go ahead and have your illusion. If you think it's fun, think that. I mean, it is, but we're just fields of energy taking on form having a human experience is all. No big deal, actually. Some folks get the frequencies all out of whack and quite frankly, they pay a big price on the physical plane. But, we can make choices, and we do, and all of our energy fields are bumping around, crashing into other energy fields and well, being human is not easy. Actually, it is a very difficult existence, if you want to know the truth."

Brooke asked, "I'm still hung up on being a Catholic in the spirit life. I would think that on the spirit side of things, there is not all the division that we have here. You mean there really is a Catholic church and a Baptist church and all the others at the spirit level?"

"Oh, no, no, no. Thanks for seeking clarification. There's none of that. There's just energy expressing itself in frequencies. I simply mean that Jim and I have this thing going. It's just something between us that gives us some fun, is all."

"But it bothers Jane," Luciano reminded Cliff.

"Well, I can't keep both of them happy."

"So, you choose to make a Catholic priest your choice for pleasing over me, saint that I am for bringing you joy for all of these years?" Jane responded, full of indignation.

Brooke and Luciano knew that they had just walked smack dab into the middle of a potential domestic spat.

"Listen, my precious Jane. I love you more than anything. You know that. This friend of mine, Jim, he gets his kicks from finding converts. I let him have his fun. It brings him joy. I can bring you joy in so many other ways, but I can only bring him joy in this one way, other than laughing at his jokes, which really takes some doing on occasion. So, no jealousy please. Another human condition, by the way, that is thankfully absent on the next plane. Let's just leave it at that, OK, Sweetie?"

"But, Cliff, the Crucifix on the wall. I take it down and it keeps going back up. Up, down, up, down. I simply can't have a Catholic Crucifix on my wall. My Jehovah's Witness friends won't understand."

"OK, this is what I'll do. I'll tell Jim that he will have to become a Jehovah's Witness. I'll tell him this is the payment for the Crucifix on our wall and I can assure you that when you come into the living room in the morning, it won't be there. You see, you just have to know how the system works. You'll learn. You'll all learn, sooner or later, but for the moment, for all of you, it will be later."

"Before you go, Cliff," Brooke stopped the couple. "One last question, and I hope you will be very honest with us."

"Sure, shoot. How else can I be?"

"Tell me," Brooke asked, "Are you present right this minute as an energized form on the physical level as we are, a human being, or are you a spirit here on this level and as we would say, dead pertaining to your physical form?"

"Ready?"

"Yup."

"Drum roll, please. I'm both just as you are both. Do you understand?" Cliff asked.

"I think so," Brooke replied. "So, let me put it this way-Cliff Hooker, human being today, is the same Cliff Hooker that went into the Triangle on the first hole of Ghostly Links."

"Yes and no. I didn't die a human death, if that is what you're after."

"Of course he didn't die!" Jane shouted. "What do you think that would make me, besides a huge, gigantic fool? The man is alive. Look at him, flesh and blood. He's got no heart, but he's.... Whoops."

"What?" Luciano asked, catching Jane's slip of the tongue.

"Never mind, never mind," Jane repeated, amazed at what she just said. "Let's go Cliff. We have to go and I mean right now! I gave in to you last time, now you give in to me. Move!!"

"Yes, Jane." Cliff looked at us, raised his hands as if to say, what can I do, but then he pointed to his chest and without voice and using exaggerated lip movements "said" I have no heart. Then Cliff gave a big cheesy grin and gave a thumbs up sign.

As the two walked out, Brooke and Luciano sat there amazed, stunned over what they had just heard.

❦

That afternoon, the high school baseball coach, with a few minor league scouts in the bleachers, took the players through some drills. Following the drills was a pickup game. Rick was asked to pitch for a group of guys not considered to be in the running to make the team.

Rick took the mound and threw a couple of warm-up pitches. He felt good. He seemed to have the confidence needed to get the ball over the plate consistently. The scouts began to notice. One scout from a minor league team owned by the New York Yankees held a speed indicator and passed the word among the scouts that young Putterbee was throwing around 98 mph and what was more incredible was that the pitches were perfectly placed. Not one player on the first team could hit them. Two players hit foul balls, but the diamond was totally controlled by Rick and his amazing demonstration of pitching.

Ghostly LINKS

While Rick was home, beaming, and telling his mom of his startling afternoon, Brooke and Luciano were summarizing the day and admitting to each other that while it was all so interesting, nothing really fit a pattern that would give them any clue about the Triangle and its strange properties.

Luciano's thoughts turned to food to get his mind off all of the information gathered during the day. "May we share dinner this evening?" he asked Brooke.

"Not this evening, Luciano. I promised Larry that I would spend the evening with him, plus it will give me a chance to try and get information out of him which will help us tomorrow. Sorry. Do you have some alternative plans?"

"I have some research articles in my valise that tangentially relate to all of this. So while you talk to Mr. Ball, I'll pour over this material and then tomorrow morning we can compare notes. Is that the plan?"

"Yes, sounds good. I simply can't handle any more information for a few hours. I'm going home and take a nap. Can I take you to your hotel, or did you rent a car at the airport?"

"No, I came in by cab. Taking me to my hotel would be most kind of you. Are you sure you wouldn't stop in for a drink?"

"No, thanks. I'm really exhausted and want to rest before dinner with Larry. I'm sure you understand."

"Yes, definitely. I'll see you in the morning and we'll hopefully make some progress on this interesting situation."

"Yes, I'm sure we will. Good night, Luciano."

Chapter Eleven

Brooke's dinner date with Larry was at 8:00. He was picking her up and taking her to dinner and then perhaps some wine and light music at Brooke's place.

Brooke took a short nap. It had been a long, emotional day with much information to process and record. She lay on a chaise lounge on her porch and quickly fell asleep with Lucky comfortably lying on the floor beside her.

Awakening from her nap, Brooke glanced at the clock. She needed to get ready for her evening with Larry. She laid her outfit on her bed and jumped into the shower. Within the half hour she was refreshed and looking very nice for her dinner date with the man she loved dearly.

As the clock struck 8:00, the door bell rang. Brooke opened the door and there was Larry looking great wearing slacks and a polo shirt.

"Hi Larry," Brooke said with a warm smile.

"Hi. You look great, Brooke."

"Oh, thank you so much, Honey." Brooke gave Larry a hug and held him in a tight embrace followed by a kiss. "Let's enjoy the evening."

Ghostly **LINKS**

Larry had ordered fine wine at an exquisite French restaurant, Le Petit Auberge. The atmosphere was Parisian. The garcons spoke French, but it was usually only for a few minutes of ambiance and to impress the guests.

The sommelier presented a decanter of Chablis Grand Cru wrapped in a towel and set in a bucket of ice. Larry and Brooke sipped a glass of wine, which included a toast to a perfect evening and then surveyed the menu. Brooke trusted Larry's judgment and asked him to order for her. Larry ordered Coquilles St. Jacques Provencale for the two of them.

The conversation temporarily turned to the case. Larry asked, "So, how is your research coming? Do you have an explanation for all of this ghostly stuff?"

"It would be safe to say that we aren't close, but today we certainly had an earful. Something is out there, Larry, but we're a long way from explaining things."

"What are you learning?"

"Well, I'm sure you'll understand, but we told the people that everything they told us would be confidential and would not go out of the room. As much as I'd like to share what I know, I simply can't."

"That's fair."

"I'm glad you understand. I feel you have a right to know; after all, these are experiences that have happened at your country club. But, these folks need to know that I keep my word when it comes to confidentially."

"Well, then let me ask, is there anything that you need to know from me?" Larry inquired.

"Yes, actually. I do have a few questions," Brooke replied.

"I figured you would."

"I don't want this perfect evening to be consumed with talk of this case, but being with you presents a perfect opportunity to get some needed information."

"Oh, believe me, I won't let our work totally consume this evening," Larry said. "But, we can talk about this and get it out of the way."

"My first question is, why was this Triangle left undeveloped in the first place?"

"The designer simply had a strong feeling about the area. I

don't know if he came under any spell or influence of the force there. But he went over the entire area and when he presented his layout of the course, there was a definite triangle on the borders of the first, eighth and ninth holes. On the blueprint, the area was encapsulated with a triangle and on the form was written, 'The Bermuda Triangle of the Links.'"

"So, the designer knew something was strange, but never explained it, right?"

"That's correct," Larry said, nodding. "I suppose a logical question would be, why did he name the spot 'The Bermuda Triangle of the Links'? I don't know the answer to that question. I'm sorry."

"Did you ever see the area before it became so thick with brush and tall grass?" Brooke asked.

"No, it always looked like that."

"Did the designer or developer ever say anything about the area, anything at all?" Brooke continued with her questioning of Larry.

"The builder told his employees to stay out of the area and he made it very clear. I was told early on to stay out too. But, the only thing I can remember is someone reported seeing or entering a cave. Whether this is true or not, it has taken on truth proportions and some people, and I don't know if you heard it today or not, believe that spirits live in that cave."

"Larry, what was this before it was a golf course?"

"Many years ago, there was a mental hospital here. It was torn down in the 1970s and the land sat unused. For decades there was a spiked fence around the property, so everybody left it alone. I mean, you couldn't hunt in the area; you couldn't get in. The land was not good for any use until a developer became interested in the mid 1990s and was able to purchase all of the land from the government. This golf course was laid out and built. It has, as you know, enjoyed success as a premier golf course in the Midwest."

"A mental hospital, huh?" Brooke asked, thinking out loud.

"That's what I'm told."

"Did people die there?"

"I'm sure they did. Some people spent their entire lives

there. I would suppose that people died and were probably buried there, or if not buried, disposed of in some way."

"Is there anybody in the community who knows about this hospital when it was in operation?"

"I'm sure there are some people. I don't know anyone. You might ask at the museum or historical society. I'm sure you could find someone who used to work there, maybe somebody who is in a nursing home."

"Can you tell me who has gone into the Triangle since it has become a golf course? And, I'd like fact and rumors."

"Facts would be Eddie Hazard on the day the course opened. He disappeared. My warning signs were posted and rumors began. People were scared because Eddie has never been seen since. He lives in California according to his son, but people don't want to believe it. They think he died in there and that his ghost is present. It was after Eddie came up missing that the rumors started.

"Then there was a long time when people believed the rumors and stayed out. A couple of weeks ago, Cliff Hooker went in to find his ball. Father McDuffy, Reverend Chip Hogan, and Reverend Spiker went in a week later. Then today, Tom Green saw Rick Putterbee trip and stumble in near the apex at the 8th and 9th holes. Rick got right up and brushed himself off. Those people are what I would call fact.

"Now, rumors; well, there are a lot of those and of course, I have no idea who comes around in the middle of the night. But, to the best of my knowledge, no one has come up missing, nor has there been any media attention around ghosts and stuff like that. This really all started in the past several days. But I didn't answer your question. The only rumored one would be a man who was a guest of one of our members. He had dyslexia, I guess, couldn't read the warning signs or my release that he signed in the Pro Shop. Apparently, he walked in.

"I never heard if the Triangle affected him in any way, but I do have his name and address and phone number in the pro shop. I was afraid I might hear from a lawyer, so I took down information and had the guy give me some way to reach him. I never heard from him, his family, or a lawyer, so I suppose he is okay. I'll give you that name tomorrow. But, as I say, a lot is going on all the time and lots of people could go in and I wouldn't know about it, but I would hear about it if somebody went in and something happened to them-lawyers and the media would be all over the place as was the case with Cliff and the ministers."

The conversation was interrupted by the arrival of salads. More wine was poured, French bread was passed, and the salads were enjoyed.

During the meal, Brooke and Larry talked about their upcoming wedding and anticipated honeymoon. In the glow of candlelight, both enjoyed the delicious Provencale put before them by the most professional garcon either had ever seen. The evening meal ended when the garcon brought the dessert, Savarin Chantilly.

Just before the two were ready to leave, Larry said, "One more thing has occurred to me. I did get a phone call from a golf professional a year or two ago. He said that playing my course was indirectly responsible for his being successful on the professional golf tour. I simply told him I was happy that Ghostly Links had some part to play in his success."

"Did he say what happened that made him successful?" Brooke asked. "Can I assume it was some interaction with the Triangle?"

"No, he didn't say. However, he did say that when he won the Masters in 2006, he would establish a foundation at Ghostly Links for young people who held promise of being successful golfers. The money would be used for lessons, opportunities to play challenging courses, and college scholarships."

"You are sure he didn't mention the Triangle?"

"I'm sure he didn't. I would have remembered. I vaguely recall a very good golfer being a guest and someone saying he shot a 66 or 67 on Ghostly Links which up until that time had not been done, except by me and a few other pros."

"Well, he certainly has a high regard for your course."

"Yes. I think I received the call when I was busy with a tournament or something and I sort of put it on the back burner. There was nothing for me to do. He said more information would be forthcoming. But in thinking of strange things happening around here, I guess a guy saying he will win the

Masters in 2006 wouldn't rank with strange unless it was simply a confident young golfer wanting to help others."

"Very interesting. What was his name, Larry?"

"You know, I really don't recall. Again, I was busy. I figured I would get more information and thank him at that time."

"So, we won't know who this was until the Master's is over in 2006."

"I guess so."

"Thanks for remembering this event. Can you go back to your guest book or talk to anyone who played with him when he got this great score?"

"As I recall they were here as guests of someone who isn't a member anymore. I really can't identify him. I'm sorry, dear."

"That's OK; thanks for relaying the story. If we don't have this solved by April of 2006, I'll know who to interview."

"Brooke, I'm hoping you can solve this mystery soon. I've got to take some action in a responsible way because the interest in this thing is getting out of hand," Larry said.

"I'll give it all I've got, Larry. We're making a little progress. I want to contact someone who knew about the mental hospital that used to be on the property and this cave needs to be investigated. Oh, and while I said I could not reveal anything to you that was said in the interviews, I will share one interesting piece of information."

"What's that?"

"There are no golf balls in the Triangle," Brooke admitted.

"Really? I thought the place would look like the aftermath of a hailstorm."

"Nope. None to be found, at least that's what we were told."

"Who told you that?"

"Once again, I want to tell you, but I can't. I thought that was an interesting piece of information that you might like to know. I felt I could tell you that without violating any confidentiality."

"Hmmm, that means they're collected. The Triangle gets every major slice on number 1, 8, and 9. My guess, on a good day, is that at least 20 balls would be hit into the Triangle and that is a very conservative estimate. That means, on a very good week, 140 balls, and in a very good month, 560 and for a

7-month season it could be around 4000, I figure. They all have to go some place. Hmm, very interesting. Maybe a home owner on the periphery of the course is going in in the middle of the night to collect them?"

"Periphery of the course. That's a group of people I didn't think to interview," Brooke said.

"You really should interview Doc Eagleton. He's quite interested in the Triangle. He reads all those flying saucer books and is quite taken with stuff like that. He has a large window in his family room and he has a very powerful telescope that he keeps trained on the Triangle."

"You've seen it, I take it?"

"Yeah, he had me over for dinner one evening. Doc is convinced that something is at work and he's looking forward to finding out what it is. I'm surprised that he wasn't one of the people who responded to the opportunity to talk to you and Luciano. I assume he didn't come in. If he did, he would have stopped in to say hello; he always does."

"Nope, he didn't call or come in."

"Well, you need to talk with him. He might have nothing to share, but on the other hand, he might have seen something. His is the closest home to the Triangle at about two hundred yards and his house sits up on a cliff so he has an excellent view of the Triangle. I can give you his phone number tomorrow."

"Great."

"Let me ask if you could reveal another finding. Is the place covered with coins?" Larry asked.

"Coins?"

"Yes, most golfers throw in quarters or some coin to appease the golf gods," Larry explained.

"Really?"

"Yeah, another crazy rumor. We had a woman visitor who got a hole in one on the seventh hole. She told a newspaper reporter that she threw a silver dollar into the Triangle on the first hole wishing for some good luck. Well, once that got around, almost everyone throws in some change for good measure. I've seen some guys stand back and heave a coin like George Washington trying to get it across the Delaware. People are funny. But, I was wondering, if this person you interviewed who said there were no golf balls said the place looked like Fort Knox."

"He didn't say."

"Hmmm, he didn't say? Well, now your confidentiality is slipping a bit since the source is now a male."

"Yup, you're a good listener, honey. That slipped away. I was imagining a collection of money on the floor of the Triangle a few inches deep. I'm sure, that if a whole lot of money were lying around in there, my interviewee would have said something about it. So, my guess is that as the golf balls are collected, so is the money."

"But if that is so, where does it go and who collects it?" Larry asked.

"Tomorrow I will get back on the case, and hopefully I'll be a little closer to getting the answers to your questions."

Larry and Brooke left the restaurant and went to Brooke's home. She invited Larry in for wine and to relax without talk of managing a golf course or trying to uncover a mystery. Larry accepted. The couple relaxed and enjoyed each other's company into the night. It was 2:15 when Larry suggested he be on his way.

Chapter Thirteen

Tuesday, August 30, 2005

Brooke picked up Luciano at his hotel around 9 a.m. A rather tired-looking Luciano got in the car.

"Good morning, Luciano. You look like you didn't sleep well last night."

"Morning, Brooke. No, I didn't. Probably being away from my bed and the familiar surroundings of my home."

"I'm sorry to hear that. Maybe tonight will be better."

"I hope so. Did you enjoy your evening with Larry?"

"Yes, we had a marvelous evening. We went to a French restaurant. You will also be pleased to learn that Larry gave us some interesting information."

Up ahead, Luciano saw a bagel place. "Let's stop there and get some breakfast," Luciano suggested. "Perhaps you can tell me what Larry had to say in there."

The two went in and purchased chocolate chip bagels and coffee. The place was practically empty as most folks had gotten their coffee on their way to work before 8 o'clock.

While chewing a fresh bagel, Luciano asked, "What did Larry have to say?"

"Ghostly Links sits on the site of what used to be a huge mental health hospital," Brooke began. "The designer or developer was concerned about this triangle of land and named it the 'Bermuda Triangle of the Links', but I don't know why. Something had to have happened when the course was being built that caused the Triangle not to be developed. I'm planning to contact the course architect this morning."

"Did you learn anything about the cave?" Luciano asked.

"He knew about the cave, but didn't have any more information."

"Anything else?"

"Yes, I asked him if he knew anyone else who might have gone into the Triangle and today he is to give me the name and phone number of a guest who played there and apparently has dyslexia and couldn't read the warning or the release form he signed in the pro shop. Larry feared a lawsuit so he got the man's name, address and phone number. We'll contact this man too and see what he can tell us."

"Sounds like a very successful evening."

"It certainly was. Oh, yes, Larry also said that a man called, I guess it was last year, and while he didn't mention the Triangle, he did tell Larry that Ghostly Links was responsible for his success and that he would win next year's Master's Golf Tournament."

"Really? Guess I should bet on this guy in Vegas next spring," Luciano said.

"Only problem is, Larry doesn't remember his name and has no way of knowing who he is."

"I was sitting on a gold mine for a minute there."

"That's what I learned. You?" Brooke asked.

"Well, I read the research articles I told you about."

"And?"

"And there was only one that might have some connection, but I doubt it."

"What's the connection?" Brooke asked.

"The common event we heard yesterday was that nobody actually died. They are missing, but we don't have any reports of dead bodies. The second common denominator was that the person changed in some significant way, on the physical plane or another plane, regardless of what you or I might believe about that. The third characteristic is that monumental things happened in a very short period of time.

"So, I used these three common characteristics to see if the literature had any help for us and as I said, I only found one study. Actually, it wasn't a study. It was a transcription of a reporter looking into an unexplained situation."

"What did you learn?" Brooke asked.

"Well, in that experience, the victims, or the people who had gotten mixed up in the paranormal activity, all returned at a particular date and while standing at the site of the original experience, disintegrated, leaving their clothes in a heap around where they stood."

"Really? And, this didn't make 60 Minutes?" Brooke asked, amazed at Luciano's story.

"Well, it made the paranormal literature. The actual disintegration wasn't witnessed by anyone, just clothes found in these piles. I think there were eight individuals in this story. So, obviously the skeptics, and that would be the majority, think it was a prank to get attention. The skeptics are convinced that someone simply collected the clothes and put them in piles and then called the police."

"It sounds like a good Rush Week activity for a fraternity or sorority on campus, if my memory serves me from my college days."

"Yes, I would tend to agree, except that the ground underneath where the bodies disintegrated contained a gray dust-like material that after analysis was determined to be a collection of all the minerals that are found in a human body. This leads me to believe that the bodies did spontaneously disintegrate. So, this, for me, has great credibility."

"So, if past is prologue, our victims, if we can call them that, may at some point, appear together around or near the Triangle and disappear."

"Yes. If the pattern from the past is the same pattern here."

"Interesting. Well, let's go to Ghostly Links and get to work. I've got phone calls and some visits to do. What are you going to do?"

"I'm going to ask you to take me back to the hotel. I am very tired and I want to sleep. Would you do that? I'll be of more help to you if I am rested."

"Sure. I'll do my calling and see what I can learn," Brooke

said. "We'll meet for dinner, if you can share the evening meal with me. We'll discuss what I found and hopefully you'll be well rested."

"Fine, thank you. I may come over to the course this afternoon. I won't sleep all day long. Although, I might, as I sure didn't sleep last night."

Chapter Fourteen

Brooke went from the hotel to the historical society. She inquired about who in the community might be able to talk to her about the old mental hospital. She was told that there was a woman named Winnie Palmer who had been a nurse at the hospital. Winnie was living with a daughter outside of town. Brooke was given the daughter's address and phone number. Winnie would be around 100 by now, the lady at the historical society thought and may not be able to give Brooke very reliable information.

Brooke called from her car phone and was pleasantly surprised to be welcomed to visit Winnie's home. The daughter, who introduced herself as Bea, said that Winnie was awake and would be coming to breakfast in the next few minutes. Bea said Winnie would be thrilled to have a visitor.

Brooke pulled into the driveway of the quaint, but simple, ranch-style home. She knocked on the door and was invited in by an elderly woman with a beautiful smile. "You must be the lady who called a few minutes ago?"

"Yes, I am. My name is Brooke Parmore and I'm looking into the mystery at Ghostly Links."

"Yes, I've been reading about that in the paper. Come on in. Can I get you some coffee?"

"Yes, please. I like it black, no sugar or cream."

"OK."

Bea escorted Brooke into the living room. "Mother, this is Miss Brooke Parmore. She's looking into the mystery at Ghostly Links." Bea spoke in a loud voice.

"Pleased to meet you," Winnie replied and shook Brooke's hand. She had a strong grip and seemed to be in great shape for being almost 100 years old. Winnie wore a simple striped dress. Her skin was wrinkled with aging spots on her face, hands, and arms. Her hair was white and stringy.

Brooke found it interesting that Winnie was using an old ear trumpet to hear better. Brooke had not seen one of those in a long time.

"Does that thing help you much?" Brooke asked, raising her voice.

"Oh, yes, it makes things louder. I call it my tin ear. Yeah, cheap too. No batteries and it doesn't break down. I love it. Those new-fangled hearing aids cost so much and they're so tiny. All I need is a louder voice and this trumpet does the trick."

"Very interesting. When I went to college, I was going to be an audiologist and the school where I went had a large collection of those devices out in the lobby of the clinic. I don't think I've seen one since then."

"Let me know the name of that school before you go and I'll donate mine to the collection. Listen, this piece of tin has had more speech and other sounds pass through it than all of the devices in that collection combined."

"Yes, I would imagine so."

"I've used this for about forty-five years now and it still does me good. I think of it as an old friend."

"I can understand that."

Bea gave Brooke a bagel and a cup of coffee and suggested they all sit at the dining room table where Winnie was about to have a sectioned orange, coffee and a small bowl of All-Bran.

"No matter how old you get, your digestive system needs to move it along and at my age, it needs all the help it can get. Know what I mean?" Winnie said, followed by a chuckle.

"Oh yes, I sure do." Brooke found Winnie very sharp mentally.

"What brings you out here today?" Winnie asked.

"I'm investigating the mystery at Ghostly Links and I learned last night that a mental hospital used to be where the golf course is now."

"Yes, that's right. The hospital complex was all over the area that is now that golf course. That's true."

"Good. Anyway, I went to the historical society this morning to see if they could tell me who lives in the area that might remember that hospital. The lady I spoke with said you might be able to help."

"That's nice of her. There are only a couple of folks that have a connection to the hospital."

"I'm sure you have a lot of memories. I'd like to ask a few questions. May I?" Brooke asked.

"Yes, certainly. And, you tell Bea if you need your coffee warmed up."

"I will, thanks. Well, all of the attention lately seems to be around a wooded area at Ghostly Links known as the 'Bermuda Triangle of the Links.' I don't know if you know where that is, but, I'm very curious, what was on that spot when the hospital owned all of the property?"

"In the first place, the property was owned by the government, not the hospital. We were all government employees. I know what was over that spot because I was out to the golf course the year that it opened. I wanted to see what they did with all of the land. Anyway, that Triangle was next to where the hospital was, I mean the medical hospital."

"We have reason to think that there is a cave in the Triangle. Do you know where that might go, if there is such a thing?"

"A wave in the Triangle?" Winnie asked, looking confused.

"No, a cave, you know, an opening in the ground."

"Oh, a cave, I'm sorry, my ears failed me again. Well, what you call a cave is really the beginning of a tunnel. It was built under the hospital so that the medical staff and the hospital leaders would have an escape route should there be a fire, tornado, or a war. In fact, there is a whole series of tunnels under the entire hospital complex. We used them extensively in harsh winters to bring patients to the hospital or to return them to their living quarters."

"I assume people died in the hospital," Brooke said.

"Oh yes, all the time. Well, I don't mean in any abnormal way. I mean that the entire complex was huge at one time. The residents were often committed for life. Many had been abandoned by their families and had nowhere to go."

"What happened to their bodies?"

"You know, I don't know. I was a nurse, one of several, but I don't know. We all talked about a doctor doing some experiments and taking bodies into the tunnel areas, but where he took the bodies we had no idea."

"Experiments?"

"Oh my, yes. What you could get away with back in that day and age."

"Like what?"

"Well, you didn't need any permission to experiment, and as I said most of our residents didn't have family or at least we didn't know how to contact them. So, if the doctor wanted to try some experimental procedure or some drug, he would, and if the patient died, so be it. As I recall, the doctor recorded what happened as a result of his treatment. I mean, at times I thought the hospital was more of a research lab than a hospital to treat the sick and dying."

"I see. Were there other doctors there?"

"Huh?" Winnie said, leaning closer to Brooke with her ear trumpet focused in the direction of the sound.

"Were there other doctors on staff?"

"Oh yes, there were many doctors. Back then there were three 8-hour shifts. The hospital was the community's largest employer. It was practically a city there."

"Yes, I can imagine. Did the tunnels go outside the property, you know, did they extend beyond the hospital property?"

"Oh, yes, they did. One did, anyway."

"Where did it go to?" Brooke asked.

"Let's see. One went to the city building. Sometimes the sheriff would catch somebody for doing something wrong and just turn him over to the hospital. Oh my, things were sure different back then, but it was all considered okay at the time. They would go through the tunnel and come up into the hospital for our evaluation."

"That's interesting. Is that tunnel still connected to the city building?" Brooke asked.

"I'm sure it isn't. You can go over to the county jail. It's still in the same spot. I'm sure it has been cemented shut, but I don't know that for a fact. Want some more coffee?"

"Yes, thank you."

Bea, who had been listening, went into the kitchen to get more coffee for the decanter. She soon returned and poured a cup for Brooke.

"Thank you. When you were at the hospital, were there any ghostly things that went on?"

"Toasty things? What do you mean by that?" Winnie asked.

Brooke leaned a bit closer to her ear trumpet, "Not toasty things; I said were there any ghostly things that went on?"

"Ghostly, not toasty. Oh my, as I said, I can't hear very well and often I get confused. Sorry. To answer your question, yes, all the time. It got to be almost comical. We nurses would always watch for the next crazy thing to happen. After awhile you have no fear. You figured you were surrounded with a bunch of spirits and it became a way of life."

"Really? Must have been very unsettling."

"Not really. It was the way to explain strange things happening. Today I suppose folks say, 'It must be a full moon for this and that to happen,' but back then we'd say, 'Some ghost is at it again.' Nothing big mind you, just a lot of little things, like doors opening and closing with no wind or draft, pictures falling, unidentifiable sounds, hazy appearances. You know, all the traditional things attributed to ghosts."

"I think that's all I need, Winnie," Brooke said, intending to bring the interview to an end. "You've been very helpful."

"You don't want to hear the most famous of all stories at the hospital?"

"Oh, sure," Brooke replied. "I'm sorry; I should have asked if you had anything to share. Of course I want to hear about it. Tell me."

"It happened on a very stormy night. I remember that. Nobody was going out into the storm. It was one of those worst storms of the century that come along every so often.

"It was late at night. Sometimes, I worked the midnight shift for extra pay or to help another nurse who needed a break. Anyway, it was a terrible storm and all of a sudden, the lights went off, and of course, our machines shut down as well. At that time, we didn't have any lifesaving mechanical devices like they have today, so it wasn't the problem back then that it would be today, plus I hear they have some backup generators or something so they don't have to worry about losing electricity. But, I'm getting away from myself here.

"So, the lights went out. We were all in total darkness and in that total darkness the ghosts became obvious. It didn't take much energy for them to give off their distinctive ghostly appearance. That's what people see today by the way, energy that is a frequency that corresponds to our ability to see images. Anyway, there I go getting off the subject again. In total darkness we could see many ghosts. I mean it was like we were at a meeting of ghosts. We were totally outnumbered and I remember saying to someone, they must be all around here all the time. We don't see them is all."

"That must have been quite an experience," Brooke noted.

"Oh, it was. Then the lights came back on and it all seemed so normal. So, after that, whenever something strange happened, we simply accepted that it was one of those ghosts. Of course, a lot of rumors started back then and many of them were about the ghosts being souls who died in the hospital or were used in the doctor's experiments."

"Let me ask. Did any of the people working at the hospital suddenly have some ability, you know, like predict the future or play a musical instrument? Or, perhaps magically cured of some illness?"

"Well, as a matter of fact, there was what some of the doctors called 'miracles.' You know, instant healings. We would laugh many times because a patient would say, 'Hey, Doc after this operation, will I be able to play the piano?' And you know what, he or she could. It was uncanny. We even had visitors to the hospital who called to report some strange event in their lives after having visited our hospital. We thought it a coincidence."

"Hmmm, that's very interesting. Well, I don't want to overdo my welcome. I guess I'll be going. You've been most helpful, Winnie, and thank you, Bea, for your hospitality and coffee."

"Please come and visit again, Miss Parmore, and be sure and tell us what you learn, okay?"

"Yes, I will." Brooke walked to her car and drove down the road to talk to the county sheriff and see if such a tunnel existed.

Bea said to Winnie, "She seemed like such a nice person."

"Yes, very nice."

"Thanks for not telling her I was a patient at the hospital and that I am a ghost, Winnie. I so appreciate your kindness."

"I know you do, Bea."

⚜

While Brooke was talking to Winnie and Bea, Larry was being visited by Professor Isaac Divotski and two graduate students from the University: Tom Rodriguez and Cheri Webb. They had read the *Gazette* and gotten caught up in all the frenzy around the Bermuda Triangle on the Links. A technology class project became how to explore the Triangle without putting any human in jeopardy. The three sat in the conference room with Larry and began to share their plan for exploration of the Triangle.

When Professor Divotski and the students arrived at Ghostly Links, they saw a sign by the entrance. In big red letters was SPOOKTACULAR GOLF OUTING—DON'T MISS THIS YEAR'S OUTING!

Once inside, the professor asked Larry, "What is a 'Spooktacular Golf Outing?'"

"Biggest event of the year. The members go all out and have a good time. The committee uses the ghost theme and imaginations run wild."

"I'm sure food is a draw?"

"Absolutely. They serve Ghost Burgers. They claim they are so good they disappear before you realize you have one in your hand. Then they serve Freaky Fries—they look like French fries but taste like American fries. A favorite is Haunting Salad; the ingredients leave you wondering what was in it. Most stay away from the Boo Beans, they instantly go from a solid to a gas! For dessert the guests receive Creepy Cookies. These are chocolate chip cookies with no chocolate in them."

"I see what you mean by using the imagination."

"We have lots of contests too."

"Like a hole in one?" the Professor asked.

"Yeah, except in ours you win by being on the green but farthest from the pin. The theory is that the ball would have gone in the hole, but the ghostly influence kept it away."

"Cool. What other contests do you have?"

"We have the longest drive, but we subtract 20 yards from the point where the ball stops because we believe a ghost simply pushes the ball along about 20 yards or so."

"You guys think of everything."

"We try to. It is all based on having a good time. There are games for the kids, prizes for the best ghost costume, best scream, and best ghost story. The committee works all year long to put on a fantastic fun day for all of the members."

After this break-the-ice dialogue, the professor began to try and convince Larry that their robot could be useful to him.

"The way we see it Mr. Ball, a way to effectively inspect the Triangle would be to send in a robot with a TV camera on it," Professor Divotski began. "The camera would rotate giving you a 360 degree view of the Triangle area. Since the robot is all mechanical parts, you could see as well as analyze what happens to it. The robot could travel over rocks and logs and has the capability of going around trees and through marsh."

"This is the safest type of surveillance," Tom Rodriguez offered. "This is the same technology that goes into areas where bombs have the potential of exploding."

"The technology allows us to be fail safe in the sense that no human can be harmed," Cheri Webb added. "We can use it at any hour and it has quite a bit of power which gives it a significant amount of time to be in the Triangle."

"We'd really like to experiment, Mr. Ball. What can we do to convince you to give it a try?" Professor Divotski concluded.

"I need to check this out with others," Larry replied. "I won't authorize it without talking to my advisors, but I will say that it makes sense to me. I really don't see why you couldn't do this, but you'll have to wait till I give you a green light."

"We understand," Professor Divotski said. "We'll await your call and if your advisors have any questions, just let me know. Oh, the robot can take something in and leave it as well. It can also bring things out, sort of like the robot on the moon brought rocks out. It is very versatile. And, we think your problem is a perfect use of this technology."

"Thanks," Larry said. "I'll be in touch."

As Larry walked to his office he knew that his advisor would have no problem with it. His advisor was really Brooke Parmore. If Brooke wanted it to happen, it would. If she had problems with it, there would have to be a delay.

Chapter Fifteen

While Larry was talking to the professor, Brooke was across the desk from County Sheriff Eric Woodrough. She explained the purpose of her visit.

"I've learned this morning that years ago there was a tunnel from the mental hospital to places outside of their property. My source is very certain that there is a tunnel from what is now the Bermuda Triangle of the Links to your building here. Do you know anything about this?"

"Oh, yes. I sure do."

"That's good. I feared you wouldn't have a clue that this existed many years ago."

"Oh, no, we're up to speed on this problem."

"Problem?" Brooke asked.

"Yes, problem. And, I'm sorry that you have learned this because we've put more effort into cover-up than any other initiative in the department."

"Really?"

"That's right. I've lied about that tunnel for so long my Pinnochio nose is practically down to my knees. I'm sick and tired of living lies. I'm curious who told you about the tunnel, but I understand sources and won't ask you."

"Thanks," Brooke said, appreciating the lack of pressure to divulge her source.

"I know of your work and believe that you will handle this very professionally, so if you won't let the world know that I was the one to let out the tunnel secret, I'll cooperate with you."

"I appreciate it, Sheriff ," Brooke said. "All I know is that a tunnel comes to your building. I don't know what is in the tunnel."

"Neither do I. I don't know what your source told you, but it was sealed decades ago. As far as I know, it's never been tampered with since the day the concrete dried."

"Can I see it?"

"Sure. Come on, I'll show you."

The two went down into a musty and damp basement. The outline of the tunnel was obvious when Sheriff Woodrough shone his powerful flashlight onto the wall.

"Why have you had to lie so much?" Brooke asked. "I don't understand. All we have is a tunnel that was sealed years ago. So what?"

"It isn't so much that there was a tunnel, it's what is rumored to be happening on the other side."

"What can you tell me about that?"

"Let's get out of here and return to my office."

The conversation continued in Sheriff Woodrough's office. "The lie that I have kept telling is that that tunnel entrance is the only passage into the hospital underground tunnel network."

"There's another entrance?"

"Yes, there is."

"In this building?"

"In the building that is attached to this building. It is a part of a jail cell."

"A jail cell?" Brooke asked, somewhat surprised.

"Yes, we put our most hardened criminals in there."

"The guy in jail goes into the tunnel?" Brooke asked.

"Well, sometimes, but it's not very often. You see, this jail cell has as much of a reputation among criminals as the Bermuda Triangle of the Links has with golfers."

"That's interesting."

"Yeah, so on a rare occasion if the criminal is desperate or curious he'll try to get out."

"Where does he go?" Brooke asked.

"No idea."

"Hmmm, interesting. The guy just disappears? I still don't get what you have to lie about?"

"The question asked is, 'For those who go and don't return, what happened to them?' Attorneys need to see them; judges want to know what happened to them. The media wants to report escapes from jail and there aren't any. I need to protect the integrity of my staff. Listen, I've been very creative in my explanations. You wouldn't believe some of the stories I've concocted."

"Can I see this cell?"

"Yeah, try not to pay much attention to the guys in jail. They may whistle or say something you'll find offensive."

"Thanks."

As the two were making their way to the jail cells, the sheriff explained what he knew. "What happened was this, and what I'm about to say has been passed down for decades. When the doc at the hospital couldn't handle some guy, he'd cover his face with an ether mask, put him in a wheelchair and wheel him to this cell. In a sense, this cell was the hospital's maximum security cell. Then through an agreement with the sheriff at that time, the guy would be in jail and not be a problem to the hospital. This way they didn't have to go through procedures.

"It worked the other way too. If the sheriff got a guy who wasn't violent, but a problem to society, he'd put him in the hospital cell and the doc would come over, knock him out with ether and take him into the hospital and keep him there. This kind of back and forth trading went on all the time.

"About 50 years ago when the hospital was torn down, there was a revolving panel built at the back of a cell. The only control for this panel to revolve was from some force on the other side. The panel never opened when an officer was down there. When the opening occurs, the prisoner has to decide if he thinks freedom is a tunnel walk away or whether he will stay put.

"When I became sheriff, I tried to seal the tunnel, but every time I had it sealed, the thing came down. To this day, that panel will be opened by some force on the other side and a prisoner is challenged to try and make it out or to remain in the jail cell."

"Why don't you just not put anyone in that call?" Brooke asked.

"Oh, I didn't make something clear. I'm sorry. All the cells would open and any prisoner could go into the tunnel."

"I see, that makes it clear. Did anyone see any ghosts?"

"Oh, yes, whenever the panel would open, the room would be invaded by ghosts. I had one prisoner tell me it was like being in bat-filled Carlsbad Caverns out in New Mexico. They were all over and even talking to the guys. Many would freak out.

"Now the reason none of this ever came out from the guys in jail was that to a man, each felt that telling anyone about this would give them another label, 'crazy' and a guy with a record doesn't want 'crazy' on his head because then you might go to the mental hospital and I'll tell you this, a prison compared to a mental hospital is like a country club compared to a run-down public course. There simply is no comparison. So, to keep our sanity, we just play along and I did my best to explain the disappearance of an occasional prisoner, but that was up until today.

"I'm all finished. I'm now working with you to straighten this all out, to come clean and get a new start in life. If I'm fired or not re-elected, so be it, peace of mind is far more important than the stress of living lies."

"I appreciate your telling me all of this," Brooke replied thankful for the information. "It certainly adds a new dimension to the case."

"You tell me what I need to do and I'm your man," Sheriff Woodrough said, eager to have this mystery solved.

"OK, here's my card," Brooke said. "If I can have yours, we'll keep in touch."

❧

Larry met with Clarence Shank following the meeting with Professor Divotski and his students. Larry explained that Clarence was recommended as a fine marketing resource. Information about the Bermuda Triangle of the Links was presented. Clarence agreed with the marketing professor that Larry was sitting on a gold mine.

Larry and Clarence discussed several options such as tours, a museum, a website, a foundation, and a book about the Triangle. Clarence promised, for a fee, to develop a report for Larry's consideration. The report would be a detailed plan of how to maximize this phenomenon while allowing the golf course to remain separate.

The two agreed upon a one-month timeline for the report. The report was also to explain how the plan could be operational immediately as each day that money was not coming in was wasted opportunity. Clarence and Larry shook hands, and Clarence left to begin his work.

⚜

Brooke went to the Ghostly Links course. It was approaching noon. She wasn't hungry as the bagel and the coffee at Winnie's seemed to be holding off any hunger pains.

Brooke appeared at Larry's office. "May I say, once again, Mr. Ball, thank you very much for last evening? I love every minute I'm with you."

"The feeling's mutual," Larry said with a smile, as he approached Brooke and gave her a light kiss on the cheek.

"How has your work been going this morning?" Larry asked.

"Very good. There are a series of tunnels under your course that in their day provided an underground network of travel for hospital staff and some tunnels went outside the hospital grounds."

"Really? That's interesting. I hadn't heard that."

"Yeah. I talked to a delightful elderly woman who used to work at the hospital. I also talked to the sheriff because one of the tunnels used to come up in the County Building."

"Hmmm, County Building. That's interesting. Wonder why?" Larry asked.

"I don't know. Another tunnel went to the jail. Patients and prisoners used to be sent back and forth between the two buildings."

"A lot of things like that probably happened back then."

"Can you give me the name of the guest who wandered into the Triangle," Brooke asked. "Remember, the man with dyslexia? I also need the phone number for Doctor Eagleton."

"Right. Here it is. His name is Bob Rule, not a very difficult name to remember. He lives in Chicago and the phone number is area code 889-555-5997. And, here is the number of Doc Eagleton," Larry said, giving Brooke a slip of paper with the numbers on it.

"Thanks, Larry. I'll call them right now. It's close to eleven in Chicago. Maybe I'll be lucky and get through. Do you know his line of work?"

"No, I don't. Can't help there."

"I'll go into the conference room and call."

"Can we have dinner again tonight, Brooke?" Larry asked.

"I promised Luciano that I'd have dinner with him. He's come here to help me and I shouldn't leave him on his own two evenings in a row."

"I understand. I'll give you a call later tonight."

Brooke went into the conference room and dialed the number for Bob Rule.

After two rings she heard, "Rule Industries. How may I direct your call?"

"I'd like to speak to Mr. Bob Rule, please."

"May I tell him who is calling?"

"Sure, my name is Brooke Parmore."

In a matter of seconds, he was on the line. "This is Bob Rule."

"Mr. Rule, good morning. This is Brooke Parmore and I'm calling from the Ghostly Links Country Club. I understand you played the course in the past."

"Yes, I did. It's a championship course."

"I hope you scored well?"

"As a matter of fact, I did quite well. How can I help you?"

"I'm investigating a case and have contracted with a well-known expert in the area of paranormal psychology, Dr. Luciano DiNatale. We've had some people go into the Bermuda Triangle of the Links and it has caused quite a stir in the community."

"What do you think I can help you with?"

"We understand that while you were here, you may have inadvertently gone into the Triangle. So, I'm calling to see if you would be willing to talk about your experience?"

"It was a memorable day. I've not said anything about that day to anyone except my doctor. I don't know you. For all I know I may be talking to a writer for some crazy tabloid and if that is true, I won't want to say anything."

"I understand your apprehension, Mr. Rule. Your name was given to me by the head golf professional, Larry Ball, and I can only ask you to trust that I am a professional investigator and will keep whatever you tell me in confidence."

"I'll tell you what; if you are willing, I can either bring you to Chicago on my private jet or I can fly to you. I'm willing to talk with you, but would rather talk face to face."

"Yes. Either would be fine. I very much would like to talk with you."

"We can meet in your city airport's conference room."

"That would be fine. How long would it take you to get here?" Brooke asked.

"I can be there around one or one-thirty your time."

"I'll be in the conference room at our airport when you arrive, OK?"

"Yes. That'll be fine."

"Thank you, Mr. Rule. Thank you very much."

Chapter Sixteen

Larry had forgotten to tell Brooke about the professor and graduate students from the university and their proposal to send a robot into the Triangle. He knew Brooke was on her way to the airport so he reached her on her cell phone."

"Hello. Brooke Parmore."

"Brooke, this is Larry."

"Hi, Larry. What's on your mind?"

"I forgot to tell you that I had a meeting this morning with a university professor and two graduate students. They proposed a robot be guided into the Triangle with a camera which would swivel and give us a chance to look around."

"Interesting."

"Yeah, I told him that I would have to check with my advisor, which, by the way, is you, to see what reaction I would get to the idea."

"I like it. It's an information source with no risk. If it is small enough, it could go through the tunnels, and I sure would like to see what is in those tunnels without risking any harm to people."

"Shall I tell them they're welcome to conduct their experiment?" Larry asked.

"I'd give them a positive nod, but I think we'd want to have control of the process, the information gathered, a policy of no press release and a lot of technical stuff. The last thing I'd do is turn the Triangle over to them to do whatever they wish with what they learn. We want to control it, Larry."

"Yes, definitely."

"They want an application of their technology and we have a need to learn what their product can provide for us. So, it appears to be one of those win-win scenarios, but I want control. See if they can live with that."

"OK, I'll call the professor and see what he says."

"Great. Thanks, Larry."

⚭

The corporate jet set down at ten minutes after one and taxied up to the terminal. A very fashionably dressed gentleman with dark glasses emerged from the plane carrying a briefcase. He was definitely fitting the description of a very successful CEO.

Brooke thought him handsome and that "playboy" would also be a fair descriptor for the middle-aged gentleman. She watched as he walked toward the terminal.

Mr. Rule and his entourage entered the terminal. "Hello. You must be Miss Parmore?" Bob asked, flashing a warm smile.

"Yes, and you must be Mr. Rule."

"Yes, I am. It's a pleasure to meet you." Bob introduced his personal secretary Cassandra Pepper and his pilot to Brooke. "Can I buy you a drink?" Bob asked.

"I generally don't drink when I'm working and this is business, but to celebrate our meeting, I'll take a gin and tonic. Thank you."

Bob turned to Miss Pepper and asked for Miss Parmore's drink as well as a martini, very dry, for himself. When the drinks were brought, Bob dismissed Cassandra and told her he expected to be with Miss Parmore for a short meeting and to feel free to call him at any time if, in her opinion, he needed to be interrupted. The attractive assistant walked from the room to join the pilot.

"Now, how can I help you?" Bob asked.

"Well, first, thanks for coming over here to talk with me and thanks for the drink."

"My pleasure."

"I'm investigating the mysterious experiences of people who by choice or not, enter what you know as the Bermuda Triangle of the Links at the Ghostly Links Country Club. In the course of my research, I've learned that you were one of the people who walked into the Triangle and I'm hoping you would be willing to share what happened to you, so that I can add your experience to what I am learning from others."

"I'm most happy to participate even though I will assure you that other than my doctor, you are the only one to hear what I am about to say. And, I will be very disappointed if what I tell you leaves this conference room."

"Mr. Rule, I...."

"Please, let me finish."

"I'm sorry."

"What happened to me is strange and significant. Secrets are to be kept in some quarters; lawyers and their clients, priests and their parishioners, and now you and me. Am I making myself clear?"

"I understand. You can trust me," Brooke replied. "I will keep what I hear to myself."

"I didn't know about the warning not to go into the Triangle, nor did I know what release form I was signing in the Pro Shop, because at that time, I was embarrassed by my inability to read. Since then I have no problem, as I'll explain in a few minutes. But on that day, I went into what you call the Triangle to get my ball, thinking it was simply out of bounds or unplayable. It was a brand new ball, a Christmas gift from my nephew. I thought I could find it, so I walked in.

"As I recall, and my memory is quite good, I didn't see much because of all the brush, trees, and tall grass. There was some marsh area too. But, I did see a definite outline of a ghost and he spoke to me. This will sound crazy to you but I had the feeling I was talking to the ghost of Bobby Jones."

"Bobby Jones, as in the world famous golfer, Bobby Jones?"

"Yes, as I said, just a feeling."

"He spoke to you?" Brooke asked.

"Yes. He welcomed me and seemed polite. I didn't panic. I was sort of transfixed is the way I describe it. I seemed to be in the presence of something or someone that I didn't think was human and yet talked like a human.

"The ghost-like being said, 'What do you wish for?' I repeated his question, I said, 'What do I wish for? Like you are a genie or something?' He didn't seem to see the humor in my comment. He repeated his favor; I want to give you a wish. What might it be?'

"I mean, what do you say? This is one wish. I didn't have the sense to say world peace, a cure for cancer or AIDS, free the world of hunger, anything admirable. I simply thought for a second and then offered a very selfish wish. I said, 'I'd like to know how to read and be a successful businessman making millions of dollars.'

"'It will happen,' he said, and then he vanished."

"Vanished? How did he vanish?" Brooke asked.

"Just disappeared."

"Looking at you now, I would say your wish came true."

"Yes, it did."

"Hmmm, very interesting. You went into the Triangle, encountered a ghost-like figure who granted you a wish. You stated it and it came true."

"Yes, that's correct. Now, Miss Parmore, do you understand why I can't tell anybody what happened in that Triangle?"

Brooke decided to change the subject a bit. "Your reading. You just woke up one morning and could read?"

"No, I was led to a teacher who could teach non-readers and over a short time she worked her miracle."

"Your business is highly successful?"

"Absolutely. The breaks came my way almost magically and my company is doing very well."

"May I ask you an important question?"

"Yes, sure."

"Are you a ghost now or are you a human being?"

"I am a human being, Miss Parmore. One hundred percent. Why do you ask?"

"Your experience seems to be very different from the others. Of course, I cannot share their stories just as I will not share your story, but your story is quite different, at least at this point in my research."

"I will also tell you that I have to fight the urge to go back," Bob said, looking concerned.

"Urge to go back?" Brooke asked.

"Yes, I often have strong vibrations pulling me back there. The sense I get is that there will be some type of reunion of all people who have been in the Triangle."

"A reunion?"

"Yes. It is in the future, but details have not been given to me. The impression I get is that the attraction will be great to go back and I even feel a threat may be associated with it, like I will lose all I have, or something like that. I really don't want to go, but when the time comes I may have no choice. Who knows?"

"Will you tell me when that reunion is to happen?"

"Yes, I will commit to do that."

"Thank you very much. You have helped me and I appreciate it. Here is my card in case you wish to share something else."

"I hope my information has been helpful, Miss Parmore?"

"Yes, most definitely. I can't thank you enough for sharing your story."

"You're welcome and if you are ever in Chicago, I hope you will join me for dinner at my club. The view of the Chicago skyline is out of this world on a clear night. I will treat you to an evening you won't forget. Just call and we'll have a marvelous time."

"Thank you very much, Mr. Rule."

"Bob, please."

"Fine, then I ask you to call me Brooke."

"Fine. Nice to talk with you, Brooke. Please let me know when you solve this mystery. I will be interested in what you discover."

"Absolutely. You'll be one of the first to know."

"Thank you."

Cassandra Pepper appeared, gathered up papers, and carried Bob's attaché case as the two, along with the pilot, walked out to the corporate jet. The three entered the plane and soon were lifting from the runway on their way to Chicago.

Brooke took a deep breath. It had been quite a day and it was only three o'clock in the afternoon.

Chapter Seventeen

Larry called Professor Divotski to talk to him about his plan for using a robot to explore the Triangle. He was pleased that Brooke was supportive of this idea because he firmly believed that once the inside of the Triangle could be seen, the mystery would begin to be solved.

"Good afternoon, Professor, this is Larry Ball from the Ghostly Links Country Club."

"Yes, Mr. Ball. Thanks for calling."

"I talked with my advisor and we've decided to give you and your robot a try."

"Very good. Thank you."

"There are some conditions, however."

"There usually are. That's to be expected."

"It's all about control, Professor."

"It usually is. I'll save you the request. The university is simply desirous of allowing you to use our technology to try and solve a problem. You have control of all the information we help you obtain, you own everything, make all decisions. All we desire is an opportunity to see if the robot performs in such a way that it solves a problem for you."

"That's great. If that's the case, you've got a green light."

"I will say, however, that if there is any report or any media attention, my dean would appreciate an acknowledgment."

"That's a given, Professor."

"Good. Where do we go from here?"

"I think the next step would be for you and your students to meet with Brooke Parmore and Mr. DiNatale who are investigating the mystery. It seems to me that the six of us need to sit down and talk."

"I agree. When can that happen?"

"Dinner here at the club is possible. I'll have to clear it with Miss Parmore, but a dinner meeting would be convenient. Can you and your students meet this evening?"

"Yes, I'm sure we can. This is an important project for us."

"Plan to be here at 7:00. I'll need to clear this with Brooke and Luciano. I'll call you if this time won't work."

"That's fine. May we bring the robot to demonstrate its capabilities?"

"Sure, that'd be fine."

Larry reached Brooke who agreed to the meeting with the professor and others at 7:00. She learned from a message on her answering machine that Luciano had been meeting with the Hookers in the afternoon and would look forward to talking with her around the dinner hour.

⚜

While Luciano was resting in his hotel room, he had the thought to talk once more to the Hookers. Cliff not having a heart intrigued him such that he was compelled to learn more. Luciano was seated at the dining room table in the home of Cliff and Jane Hooker.

"Thanks for your willingness to meet with me," Luciano said.

"You're welcome," Jane replied. "I don't know what more we can tell you, but if you have questions, we'll do our best to answer them."

"Thank you. Jane, I know you became quite upset when we learned that Cliff has no heart, but that was perhaps the most important piece of information we received yesterday, based on all of our interviews. It is absolutely critical that we understand this so we can solve this mystery. I beg of you to tell me what happened."

"I suppose it's all right." Jane said. "I probably have been unwilling to face reality since the day Cliff walked into the Triangle. I'm having so much trouble adjusting to everything that has happened. But, I guess, we do need to help you so others can be spared an upsetting experience. I do not object to your knowing more about this."

"Thank you. Please tell me about not having a heart, Cliff."

"Well, nothing much to tell. We discovered it in my doctor's office, the same day of my walking into the Triangle. We went to the doc and she confirmed it by X-ray and an EKG read-out."

"Some detail, please. There is no heart in your body, or is the organ there, but not working?"

"There is no heart in my body."

"But, the blood. How can it be moving to support your physical body?"

"I have a chip implanted in my back."

"A chip?"

"Yes, I've never seen it, but my doctor has. She says it is a postage-stamp-size chip that she thinks controls the blood moving through my body."

"Why do you think this has happened, Mr. Hooker? Were you worried about your heart? Had you had a heart attack?"

"At that time, I was very large, weighed more than 350 pounds, I think. I had had a heart attack a year ago and had a bypass, but I just couldn't discipline myself with my compulsive eating. I knew I was literally killing myself but I so enjoyed the food that I guess I accepted the obvious consequence. It was a choice I made. I am probably no different than the millions of smokers who are simply looking death in the eye—just a matter of time. So, yes, I did not have a good heart. I wished I could be slim and healthy, but simply couldn't put any will power to work."

"You wished for good health?"

"Yes, don't we all? If you have your health, you have it all."

"Yes, that's true."

"I wonder if any other person who went into the Triangle had an organ removed and a chip inserted in their body."

"I can't help you there. I have not even talked to another person who went in, except for Father Jim, but we don't seem to be able to talk about our experience in the Triangle. Maybe I will someday. That might be an interesting reunion. I mean, we're a rather unique fraternity of people."

"Yes, you are," Luciano replied. "You have a good idea, though. Bringing people together to talk and share their experiences. I'll mention that to Miss Parmore and see what she thinks of the idea. Thank you."

"Glad to help."

"If you think of anything else you'd like to share with us, please call me at the hotel, I think I gave you the number yesterday."

"Yes. We have it."

"Good."

Luciano thanked Jane and Cliff for their willingness to share additional information. He called for a cab, and having received a message from Brooke about dinner at Ghostly Links, asked the cab driver to take him directly to the Country Club.

Chapter Eighteen

While waiting for Professor Divotski and his graduate students to arrive with the robot, Brooke and Luciano noticed a large, leather-bound book in the lobby with an intriguing title, "Ghostly Experiences." Luciano opened the book and began to read it. *This must be the book Sam Player mentioned earlier,* he thought.

Luciano found an introductory paragraph and then a series of experiences that members and their guests had had while playing golf at Ghostly Links. The name, date, and experience were chronicled since Eddie Hazard walked into the Triangle the day the course opened, July 4, 1999.

The couple noted some of the more intriguing entries:

8. Long putt—going right to the hole—then veers off right before the hole. All in foursome couldn't believe their eyes! (May 5, 2000, Mike Pritchard)

21. The ball, seen by all four golfers, rolled onto the edge of the rough on the 6th hole. When the players arrived they couldn't find the ball, until Fred saw the ball up in the crook of a

nearby tree. It was his ball, because of his initials stamped on the golf ball and this was the first time he had played the course. All four were sure they heard some chuckling, but could not see anyone. (August 12, 2001, Jim Greenless)

42. A ball was floating on a pond. When it was retrieved most were sure it was a foam ball used for practice. It was a real golf ball and the pond was not the Great Salt Lake! (July 9, 2002, John Perrin)

45. On the 15th hole, a putt approached the hole. It dropped and then popped out and rested on the lip of the cup. (September 3, 2002, Ted Welgoss)

57. On the 17th tee, a driver swung and hit the ball. All saw it leave the tee box, but when the golfer bent down to get his tee, the ball was sitting on the tee. (April 30, 2003, Bruce Gardner)

69. On the second hole, two golfers approached to within five yards of the flagstick on the right side of the green. However, when the golfers reached the green, the flagstick was on the right side and there was no visible hole change on the green. (July 23, 2004, John Peace)

Larry walked up and greeted Luciano. Luciano took the opportunity to ask Larry about these fascinating occurrences. Larry said, "Well, if you knew those guys you'd take all of that with a grain of salt. Personally, I think they were simply trying to outdo each other in storytelling. The imaginations of the golfers are about as creative as the planning committee for the Spooktacular Golf Outing!"

"They make for good reading," Luciano said, smiling at the stories.

"By the way, I hope you get to play this course before you have to go back to New Jersey," Larry said.

"Thank you. I've heard so much about it, I feel like I've already played a round. I did bring my clubs. Brooke thought we might find some time."

"Just be sure to stay out of the Triangle," Larry said, with caution.

"I've actually given some thought to walking into the Triangle. Maybe I'd get my lifelong wish, a hole in one." Both men chuckled realizing that Luciano was not serious.

"You are my guest and please make time to enjoy our beautiful course. In addition to being a strange setting, it will offer you a one-of-a-kind challenge."

"Thanks for your offer. I'll keep the clubs handy in case the opportunity presents itself," Luciano said, appreciating Larry's thoughtfulness.

∗∗∗

The Professor and students arrived. They managed to bring the robot into the conference room of the Ghostly Links Country Club. The robot was a cross between R2D2 of *Star Wars* and the vacuum cleaner on *Teletubbies*. The device was relatively small. Its mechanical parts were housed in a grey metal rectangular shaped box. It moved along on a system that looked a bit like an army tank with a series of wheels and moving tracks. It had traditional antennae so as to receive its instructions from a handheld command device.

On the top of the robot was a light similar to what coal miners' have affixed to their helmets. The robot didn't have any "arms" as this particular model was only designed to inspect areas such as the inside of a nuclear power facility or some other setting where a person's health would be threatened.

The device could have arms attached, if the contractor wished to have something retrieved. But for this demonstration, Professor Divotski thought its primary use would be to simply enter the Triangle and give the investigators a visual image of what was inside.

Tom and Cheri were doing some last minute adjustments and making sure the robot would function properly when activated. The professor and students wanted their audience to be impressed with what they saw.

Larry was letting the kitchen staff know that he would be needing dinners for six and he also made it clear that once his guests arrived, he did not want any interruptions.

Brooke and Luciano were conversing in the lobby of the Country Club. Luciano appeared to be energized and feeling fine after many hours of uninterrupted sleep. The two told each other of their day's work and that they would have a chance to talk in detail following the dinner and demonstration of the robot.

Larry joined Brooke and Luciano. The three went into the conference room, shook hands and introduced themselves to the folks from the university. The six sat down to dinner. Before the sun set, plans would be made for the robot to venture into the Triangle, probably within the next day or two. The plan would also call for the robot to go into the cave-like opening as described by Bob Rule and to follow the tunnel as far as images from the robot proved to be helpful.

Following dinner and a relatively long discussion of the robot's capabilities, Professor Divotski and his students took the device out onto the golf course and allowed Brooke to use the joy stick to guide the robot around the grounds. She felt like a kid with a radio-controlled car watching it speed along a driveway. It was fun.

Luciano took a turn and learned how to activate the light and the camera. They had talked earlier about trying to use film that would pick up vibrations in total darkness thinking if ghosts were present, their images would come onto the screen.

Larry was given the controls and was taught how easy it was to move the robot here and there. All could see that it had the capability of entering a tunnel or going into a cave. The spotlight would allow the person controlling the device to see what was ahead, and they would record what the robot passed as well as what was ahead. If they wanted to hear any sounds, a microphone could be turned on so that people could listen as well as see what was in the Triangle.

Cheri Webb said, "This fella needs a name." As soon as Cheri said that, Brooke spoke up, "Casper!" People chuckled and the name stuck.

Once the demonstration was over it was agreed that the first voyage of the robot would be tomorrow afternoon about three o'clock. Nothing would be said to the media and the robot would be in a truck that would back up to the Triangle where Cliff Hooker believed he walked in. It was also agreed that Larry and the graduate students would remain at the truck and discourage any curious golfers or others from hanging around.

The evening ended with firm and thankful handshakes. Larry believed that he was close to an explanation of this weird phenomenon on his course, Brooke and Luciano were of the belief that answers were waiting inside the Triangle and the robot would be their means to solving the mystery. The professor and students could see dollar signs and much discussion in the professional literature about the pragmatic use of this robot to observe and record paranormal happenings all around the world.

People went to bed with the Bermuda Triangle of the Links still unexplained, but Brooke and others felt that some answers were imminent.

Chapter Nineteen

Wednesday, August 31, 2005

Brooke couldn't get to sleep. She wished she were in Larry's arms and almost called him, but didn't. She was tired, it had been a very long and productive day, but for some reason she couldn't fall into a restful sleep.

She kept going back to yesterday morning's talk with Winnie Palmer. She went over and over her words. She realized that she should have asked about the doctor that Winnie had mentioned. Winnie didn't talk about doctors she talked about <u>a</u> doctor.

Brooke needed to know more about the doctor who conducted the experiments, the doctor who could do the experiments without permission or any procedures of ethics. Who was this doctor and where was he? First thing in the morning, she would contact Winnie Palmer and seek clarification. Having determined a course of action, Brooke drifted off to sleep, with Larry seemingly always on her mind.

✤

Two nights in a row without several hours of sleep caused Brooke to sleep until almost 9:00. Luciano had left a message saying he would be in the hotel lobby reading research. He asked Brooke to stop by and get him whenever she was able to do so.

Brooke picked Luciano up about ten o'clock. On the way to the hotel she called Winnie on her cell phone. She asked for permission to come over one more time and apologized for any inconvenience another visit would cause. She also asked permission to bring Luciano with her. Permission was granted and the two would be expected at Bea's home around 10:30.

Brooke briefed Luciano about Winnie on the way to their meeting. Brooke entered the driveway. She brought her dog Lucky with her today. Lucky didn't like being left alone so Brooke cracked the window, and like a mother, told him to behave and be quiet.

Bea had the door open and warmly welcomed Brooke and Luciano to her home.

Brooke introduced Luciano to Bea and then to Winnie who was sitting in a comfortable chair in the living room.

"Good morning, Miss Parmore, so good to see you so soon. I must not have given you all you needed a couple of days ago," Winnie said.

"Oh, yes. You did a marvelous job, but I couldn't get to sleep last night thinking about something you said. I need some clarification, please."

"Sure. I'll help if I can," Winnie said.

"Would you like some coffee or tea," Bea asked. "I made some tea this morning, a new blend from the Orient."

"I'll take some coffee," Brooke said.

"I'll try some of your tea," Luciano said. "That sounds refreshing."

Bea went to the kitchen to get the drinks for her guests.

"Yesterday morning, you mentioned a doctor who did experiments at the hospital," Brooke began, speaking toward the opening of Winnie's ear trumpet.

"Yes, I did."

"I failed to get some clarification about that. Was there only one doctor who did these experiments or did all the doctors do them?"

"There was only one. At least, I should say, as far as I recall, there was only one."

"Do you remember his name?"

"Let's see. His name was ...."

"It was Samuel Sister," Bea interrupted, coming into the room with the drinks.

"Yes, Dr. Sam Sister. That's right. I knew Bea's memory would be better than mine."

"Is he still living?" Brooke replied with a question.

"Oh, yes, very much so. A small group of hospital retirees still meet once a year for a potluck and Dr. Sam always sends a nice card with regrets that he cannot attend, but he wishes us well."

"Where does he live?" Brooke asked.

"I think he lives in, let's see, senior moment here except with me it is a double senior moment. I'm so old that I get extra credit for senior moments. He lives in ...," Winnie tried to recall.

"He lives in Canada, Sudbury, Canada." Bea once again provided the answer.

"Yes, Sudbury. I knew it had something to do with cleaning. It's my association technique for remembering things. I think he lives in a nursing home in Sudbury."

"Why Canada?" Luciano asked. "Is that his home? I mean nothing wrong with living in Canada mind you, just curious."

"He went too far with his experiments and he didn't realize that a patient in the hospital was the son of a very wealthy East Coast lawyer. The son died and the father was certain that Dr. Sister's experiments caused the death. So, we heard about the crisis and the next day there was no Dr. Sister. Rumor had it that he fled to Canada to escape prosecution, but nobody knew where in Canada he went. It was only after the New York attorney and his wife died that he surfaced in Sudbury."

"Do you remember the name of the New York attorney?"

"Oh, it was big news when it happened, but no, that name escapes me right now."

"Ronald J. Weathers, Esquire!" Bea said quietly but without doubt.

"Yes, Bea, thanks. Mr. Weathers. We nurses referred to him as 'Stormy Weathers' because he was so enraged at Dr. Sister for killing his son."

"Do you think it would be worth my while to try and contact him?" Brooke asked.

"I suppose so. As I recall back then, Dr. Sister was often made fun of by all of us. He bore a strong resemblance to the mad scientist with stringy hair, lots of test tubes, and a big laboratory. I think he was simply a genius who had a good heart and wanted to help people. But, he knew that a research center existed for him at the mental hospital so he somehow got a job there and then set up an extensive laboratory. He pretty much kept to himself.

"All of us knew that something was going on, especially when we saw patients being rolled into the laboratory and then after awhile being rolled back out with a white sheet over the entire body. Dr. Sister would take the body down a tunnel. We never knew where he went which was fine with us at the time, as we didn't need to do a lot of paperwork. Yes, even some paperwork was required back then, and we didn't have to bother with preparing a dead body for the morgue or burial. Actually, we were, in a sick way, sort of pleased that we were spared the work we would normally have to do when somebody died at the hospital."

"May I ask a question?" Luciano asked.

"Yes, please do," Brooke said.

"Do you know if any patients who were treated at the hospital are still living and especially anyone still living in this area?"

Bea rose and went into the kitchen as if to get more cookies but in reality she couldn't bare to be present when talk was going on about patients at the hospital. It was much too painful. She left the room, but not in a way that the others would suspect that anything was amiss.

"Let's see. Mental health carried such a stigma then, and even today, although it is much better today than in the past. People wouldn't be very pleased if I told you their names, but yes, there are a few in the area. I'm sorry; out of respect for their privacy, I can't tell you their names."

"I understand and respect your decision," Luciano said.

"What? Sorry, I didn't hear you," Winnie said, once again positioning her ear trumpet a little closer to Luciano.

"I said that I understand and respect you for withholding the information."

"Good. Is there anything else I can help you two with?"

"I don't think so. I do want to try and find Doctor Sister in Sudbury and I'm glad to know that there are some people in the area who were patients in the hospital. We would like to talk to somebody to see what they recall of the tunnels and Dr. Sister."

"Well, search as you might, I can assure you that nobody will know anymore than I do, except Dr. Sister. I don't say this to stifle your search, but I think it will be in vain, because I know who they are and they simply don't have any information about the tunnels or Doctor Sister or anything, for that matter. They came, were treated or I should say, housed, and then released if they could be. If they couldn't, they usually ended up in one of Doctor Sister's experiments and then died or were discharged with a claim to having been cured of their mental health problem."

"When Doctor Sister left, I assume the experiments stopped," Brooke concluded.

"Yes, as far as I know they did."

"No, they didn't!" Bea shouted from the kitchen.

Winnie was shocked that Bea said this. Winnie had decided that Brooke and Luciano had heard enough and because she didn't want any more questions, she decided to tell a fib and she did, but for some reason Bea kept the discussion going.

Winnie needed to defend herself. "Well, I don't know what Bea knows. As far as I was concerned the experiments ended."

Brooke rose and walked toward the kitchen. Luciano chatted with Winnie while Brooke conversed with Bea.

"Were there more experiments, Bea?" Brooke asked.

"Yes, his nurse carried on with his work."

"His nurse?"

"Yes, Winnie."

"You are Winnie's daughter, correct?"

"That's the cover. I have a brother, though I've never seen him."

"Cover?" Brooke asked astonished.

"To the world, I am her daughter, but the truth is that I am one of the experiments of Dr. Sister and Winnie."

"One of the experiments?"

"I probably shouldn't say anymore, Miss Parmore."

"Are you a ... should I say ... ghost?" Brooke asked bluntly.

"I can be," Bea replied.

"Can be, meaning you can choose to be a ghost or a human?"

"Yes. That was the experiment. They perfected it finally, or at least Winnie perfected it after Dr. Sister left for Canada."

"Bea! Bea!, Bea! Come here," Winnie shouted in fright.

"OK! Coming!" Bea shouted. Bea and Brooke could tell that something was terribly wrong.

❧

Brooke and Luciano were asked to leave. Winnie and Bea begged for some privacy and of course, Brooke and Luciano complied. After all, they were guests. They thanked both women for their help and quickly walked to Brooke's car. As the car pulled away, Brooke said, "What happened?"

"I praised her for her tea. Then instantly she looked horrified and shouted for Bea."

"That's it, praised her tea?"

"Yeah. I said something like, 'You did a beautiful job making this tea.'"

"Was she using her ear trumpet?"

"No. What has that got to do with it?"

"I think she heard, 'You did a beautiful job making Bea.' If I'm right, I have the second half of that puzzle. I suppose a mother would be proud to have such a compliment."

"Maybe, but she really did make Bea. Bea was a patient at the hospital and Winnie was Dr. Sister's nurse. When the doctor fled to Canada, Winnie kept up with the experiments and yes, she made Bea and yes she did a beautiful job. Your compliment of her tea was interpreted with her hearing loss as doing a beautiful job making Bea. You exposed her big and dark secret. She panicked."

"So, she thought I was on to her hospital creativity and once that was out, she panicked and called for Bea to assist in having us out of the house."

"Yes. And, I predict that if we call again, or go back, they will be gone and we'll never see them again."

"I agree, but I have a pretty good idea where they would go," Luciano said.

"Sudbury?" Brooke replied, with a calculated guess.

"Exactly."

"I think we need to do whatever we can to locate this Dr. Sister in Sudbury," Brooke advised. "We need to have him monitored, because a good hunch as to what will happen is Bea will drive Winnie to Sudbury to get Dr. Sister and the three of them will go to who knows where."

"Next stop?" Luciano asked.

"The sheriff," Brooke replied. "He can help to contact the authorities in Sudbury so that if Bea and Winnie do appear at the nursing home, they can be shadowed should they try to leave."

Chapter Twenty

"Two days in a row. To what do I owe the pleasure of your visit, Miss Parmore?"

"I need some help, Sheriff. First of all, this is my colleague, Dr. Luciano DiNatale. This is Sheriff Woodrough." The two men shook hands.

"I hope you don't mind me bringing my dog in. This is Lucky." The sheriff leaned down and gave Lucky a pat on the head and said, "Goin' to work with Miss Parmore today, huh, boy? You help her good, ya hear!"

The sheriff offered coffee, but neither took him up on his offer.

"We'll only be a minute," Brooke said. "We need your help."

"Anything, you name it. I told you yesterday that the cat is out of the bag now and I'll do whatever you need to help solve this mystery."

"Thank you. We appreciate that very much. I need you to contact your counterpart in Sudbury, Ontario, and ask him to monitor a man in a nursing home there."

"Name?"

"Dr. Sister. I don't know where he lives. Supposedly, he's a resident in a nursing home."

"Monitor him, because?" the sheriff asked.

"Luciano and I have come from the home of Bea and Winnie Palmer, east of town. We have reason to believe they will go to Sudbury to get Dr. Sister and then the three of them might go somewhere. I need to have the three of them followed."

"Has a crime been committed?"

"Not that I know of, but having the three of them available to Luciano and me is critical to solving this mystery. We said something a few minutes ago that disturbed Winnie and I expect they might try to get to Dr. Sister; and in her fear, we may lose our best clue to the mystery. You law enforcement folks help one another, don't you?"

"Yes, we sure do. There's usually a lot of red tape, but since no crime is alleged to have been committed and since you don't want an arrest or anything like that, just a tracking in the event some people move around Canada, I can ask for that help. Do you want me to do it right now while you're here, or can I handle it when you leave? It will take them several hours to get to Sudbury, if they leave soon."

"Several hours as humans in a car, but seconds in the form of ghosts," Luciano said.

"I don't understand what all this is about, but I'll call right now."

"Thank you."

The sheriff looked up a number in a directory and called. The constable in Sudbury assured the sheriff that Doctor Sister would be monitored and that if anyone came to visit, he or she would be monitored as well.

Brooke and Luciano thanked the sheriff, told him they'd try to explain all of this later, and then drove to Ghostly Links. There was nothing more that could be done but wait to learn if Winnie and Bea had tried to reach Dr. Sister. Brooke did try to call Bea under the pretense of asking how Winnie was doing, but there was no answer.

❦

Brooke had contacted Doctor Luke Eagleton, a retired doctor, whose beautiful home overlooked the Triangle. She had asked for permission to interview the couple to learn what they knew about the Triangle. She was invited to lunch with Doctor Eagleton and his wife Cynthia. Following a tour of their home, Brooke began. "I wanted to meet with you to explain that Dr. DiNatale and I are investigating the Triangle and hoping to find some explanation for the strange happenings there."

"I'm glad someone is doing so. It is time for an explanation," Luke said.

"Mr. Ball says you keep an eye on the Triangle and I want you to know that we will be sending in a robot with a camera attached to see what's inside."

"That's innovative. Good idea," Cynthia said.

"I am curious if either of you have any information to share with us?" Brooke asked.

"Well, there is one thing that might help you," Cynthia replied, with a hint of concern in her voice.

"Anything you wish to say will be helpful."

"Luke and I have wanted to share this with someone, but we didn't want to be hounded by the media and we never thought we'd meet anyone who would understand. You might be the right person."

"I hope so."

"Our story begins in winter. There is very little activity on the golf course in the winter. The course shuts down and the area becomes a ghost town, pun intended," Cynthia said, while chuckling. "The ghosts seem to leave the Triangle and stand around outside. I say 'stand around,' but they don't stand. There seems to be an aura of energy all about the Triangle. A neighbor has seen this and says it's only fog caused by warmer air in the Triangle. They think we're nuts.

"Anyway, the best way to describe it is to say it seems to be like a fire drill of sorts. Late at night, you can see the ghosts come out all around the Triangle. They hover around the area and then after a few minutes they all go back in, sort of like being sucked in. The colder it gets and the darker it gets, the clearer this becomes."

"Hmm, interesting. They just appear, and hover, and then go back in?" Brooke said.

"Well, that's almost all. You tell her what happened to you, Luke."

"I hope I can trust you, Brooke, if I may call you Brooke?"

"Yes, you can trust me, and by all means, call me Brooke."

"One night while the ghosts were milling about, I let our dog, an Alaskan husky who loves cold and snow, out for some exercise. He bounded toward them and then came back with an envelope in his mouth. I opened it and read what was inside. I kept it and will show it to you now." Luke left for a few seconds to get the note from the kitchen counter. He handed it to Brooke who took the note and read it.

"Oh, my goodness," Brooke exclaimed. "This is incredible. I can't believe this."

"A bit shocking isn't it?" Cynthia asked.

"To say the least," Brooke responded. "What did you do, if I may ask?"

"Well, as you can imagine, I couldn't give it to anyone and I chose not to follow the directions. I kept it and didn't do anything."

"You surely must have been tempted. Correct?"

"Oh, yes, many times."

"Nobody knows about this. Right?" Brooke asked.

"Nobody except Cynthia."

Brooke knew that she had found two people who fully supported her investigation.

❧

Brooke returned to Ghostly Links and tried to find a relative of Ronald J. Weathers, Esq. She went to the Internet and tried to find a national directory of attorneys. She found a Ronald J. Weathers III, an attorney in Boston. She reached him by phone at his law office. She took a minute to explain why she was calling and to acquaint Mr. Weathers with the mystery at Ghostly Links. Mr. Weathers did recall his grandfather's involvement with a doctor in a mental hospital in the Midwest.

Brooke began, "Thank you for talking with me, Mr. Weathers. I'd like to come to Boston to meet with you and interview you, but time is of the essence. Would you mind if I asked a few questions?"

"That's fine."

"Please don't bill me by the minute," Brooke said, tongue in cheek. "I'm not a rich woman."

"Not to worry. This is about my family and I'm glad to help. I do have a client coming to see me shortly, but, I don't believe this will take long. I don't have much information, but will tell you what I know."

"Thank you. Maybe I'll start right there. What do you know?"

"The story that has been passed down through my family is that my father's brother, who would have been my grandfather's eldest son, died at this mental hospital and apparently was a subject in some type of medical experiment that caused his death. My grandfather was furious. The story goes that he almost had a heart attack, as well as needing to be restrained by people, as he literally attacked the doctor."

"Really?" Brooke said, surprised to learn of the encounter between the two men.

"Yes. The story might get bigger than life with each telling, but there certainly was some type of confrontation. My grandfather was hospitalized in Boston when he arrived home.

"Anyway, my grandfather was an attorney, fresh out of Yale. He told this doctor that he would sue him and the state for thousands of dollars. That amount of money would be considered millions today."

"Right."

"The story goes that there was a settlement."

"Monetary?" Brooke asked.

"No, it's a settlement that to this day my family isn't sure actually occurred. This doctor, whose experiments killed my uncle, told my grandfather that he could grant him any wish. As the story goes, this doctor explained the research he was doing when my uncle died and must have convinced my grandfather of the validity of his offer - that anything he wished for would become true.

"We think my grandfather was smart enough to take the wish with an understanding that if it didn't come true, he'd hound this doctor for the rest of his life."

"What was his wish?"

"His wish was to find a cure for polio. At the time this happened, the polio epidemic was underway and my grandparents were terrified that their children would die of polio. I suppose it would be the equivalent of AIDS today. So, my grandfather's wish was for a cure for polio.

"My grandfather was assured that his wish would come true and in exchange my grandfather agreed to drop all charges. The rest is history, as they say. Dr. Jonas Salk did find the cure and the family debates to this day whether this crazy doctor in the Midwest brought this about or if he knew the cure was close. Remember, we didn't have the Internet back then or CNN. Most people were in the dark with progress in finding cures for significant diseases."

"Very interesting. Did your father contract polio?"

"No, he did not. He went to Yale and enjoyed a long career in law."

"Did you hear about any other people becoming upset when their relatives died at the hospital?"

"No, we didn't. Again, I think most people accepted hearing that a member of their family died and let it go. Having a family member mentally ill, it may have often been a blessing for all I know. But, my grandfather was very involved in finding a cure for his son, my uncle. He had researched hospitals and traveled extensively to find the best treatment. When he got word that my uncle had died, he and his small staff of lawyers took the place on like Watergate investigators did in the '70s.

"One last question, if I may?"

"Sure."

"You used the word 'crazy' in referring to this doctor. Were those the words used to describe him?"

"First of all, we all held the man in great disregard for what he did to a member of the Weathers family. But, we think he was on to something. We do recall our grandfather being quite impressed with this doctor's research, but was equally furious that his son was a victim. If my grandfather were answering the question, he'd probably call him brilliant but dangerous. Yes, I'm certain those would be his words."

"Thank you very much. You've been most helpful."

"You're welcome. Oh, will you let me know the results of your investigation? The family would be most interested in hearing what you learn."

"I certainly will. Have a good day." Brooke hung up and went to lunch, believing that one more piece of the puzzle had been added toward solving the mystery.

❦

Around 2 p.m., Professor Divotski and his graduate students, Tom and Cheri, arrived with "Casper." Only a few of the golfers on the course seemed to give it any attention. Of more importance was maintaining a handicap of respectability or challenging Ghostly Links in one way or another.

Tom and Cheri, along with Larry, drove the University truck to the site where Cliff Hooker supposedly had entered the Triangle. Larry's job would be to hold off the curious and to shout "fore" should a drive come in their direction.

The robot was taken from the truck and positioned to enter the Triangle. Professor Divotski, Brooke and Luciano, who were in the conference room of the Country Club, were given the signal that all was ready to go. A final check of instruments was done, TV camera and recording device activated, and the monitor was positioned so that the three could clearly see what Casper encountered. The video recorder was also turned on and ready to go as Larry and the students would want to see what the robot "saw" once the experiment was over.

The students and Larry were warned not to touch the robot when it came out of the Triangle. It would be guided onto the truck's lift by a radio-controlled device and taken back to the University for an analysis. Finally, all systems were go.

Casper slowly moved toward the Triangle. Like a tiny tank, it moved easily over the high grass and into the brush. Back at the conference room in the clubhouse, six very curious eyes watched the TV monitor, but saw nothing more than a human would see if he or she wandered in looking for a ball. The robot continued straight in and then Professor Divotski began rotating the camera, so views could be obtained from other areas. The camera would also look up and down, in addition to rotating like the head of an owl.

Brooke noted and mentioned to Luciano that no golf balls were seen on the ground, nor were any coins. Also not seen were bodies, bones, or dead animals. The robot continued to move like a tiny tank easily getting over fallen logs and through marshy land. Brooke exclaimed, "Look!!" There in view was the opening to a cave or a tunnel.

"Let's send Casper in," Brooke suggested.

"That's what we came here for," the professor replied.

"Make sure the microphone is on as well as the light beam."

"It is. I'll guide it right into the cave."

The room was full of anticipation with the three expecting some monster to come lurking around the corner and be in full view. Nothing so far, but a dark tunnel. There were no signs of any footprints or any indication that a human or an animal had been in the tunnel recently.

And then it happened. The sound meter showed random frequencies. They didn't represent speech or anything continuous like a hum or buzz. But there was sound, an intermittent sound that was indescribable.

"Oh, my God, look at that!" Brooke exclaimed.

"Whoa, stop Casper a minute and keep the camera focused on it. Actually, see if you can zoom in a bit."

"OK, is this better?"

"Yeah, it's much clearer now. Good job, Professor."

"Would you ever imagine you'd see such a thing?"

"Well, we expected the unexpected, so I'm not surprised, but I am intrigued, that's for sure," Brooke said, glued to the screen.

"I've never seen anything like this before. I'm very thankful we're getting this on film." Luciano said.

"The movements are what is so intriguing," Brooke said.

"Yeah, especially in light of there not being any wind in the tunnel. The movement is unexplainable," Professor Divotski said. "What do you want me to do with the robot at this point?"

"I say continue moving it forward. Could that ghost, or whatever it is, turn on Casper and come tearing out of the Triangle?" Brooke asked Luciano.

"No, that's highly unlikely. It's in a natural environment. It won't flee, or at least I would be shocked if it did so."

"What are we looking at, Luciano?" Brooke asked.

"It appears to be a ghost. He, or she, or it, looks like a very old human with skin and bones."

"What will it do when it sees Casper?"

"Guess we'll have to wait and see."

"OK, Professor, move Casper farther along in the tunnel and let's see what there is to see," Brooke directed. "Rotate the head so we can see what is behind him as well."

"OK, will do."

Brooke and Luciano continued to stare at the monitor as Casper's "head" swiveled. Behind Casper could be seen a girl, maybe a teenager, following the robot and looking curiously at it as if she had stumbled across a science experiment in operation, which is what she had actually done.

"Who is that?" Brooke asked.

"It looks like a young girl."

Brooke picked up the Walkie-Talkie. "Larry, this is Brooke."

"Yes, Brooke, how is it coming?"

"Fine, but have you or the students seen anyone enter the Triangle since you've been out there?"

"No, absolutely not. We've been able to monitor all three sides and no one has gone in."

"OK."

"Why do you ask?"

"Got something on camera that looks like a teenager and we wondered if she just wandered in and entered the tunnel?"

"Nope. No one has entered."

"Good. We'll review the tape when the experiment is over. Keep up the good work."

"Looking forward to seeing the tape and you, and not necessarily in that order."

"Thanks, see you soon."

The three kept their eyes on the teenager as she walked up to the robot and inspected it. She touched it and went around it.

"She sure is curious about Casper, isn't she?" Brooke said. "It certainly has her attention."

The robot continued on through the tunnel, until there

appeared to be a fork where the tunnel would go off in as many as four different directions.

"Which way do you want to go, Frost?"

"Frost?"

"Yes, the road not taken. Do you want to take the road less traveled? It could make all the difference," Professor Divotski said, wanting others to be impressed with his knowledge of American literature.

"How would you know which is the tunnel less traveled?"

"The one with the least amount of debris, I suppose."

"OK, sure, turn to the right, I guess."

"Let's glance back and see if that teenager is still there," Luciano suggested.

"The camera rotated and the girl was still there, but she had aged significantly. The further she went into the tunnel the older she looked.

"This is incredible. How does that happen?" Brooke asked, amazed at what she was seeing.

"I have no idea," Luciano replied. "Unless the tunnel represents some time machine where it is charged with some aging particles or molecules and the farther from the outside air the older the body becomes."

"OK, I'm guiding Casper down the tunnel," Professor Divotski said, wanting to draw all attention to the video screen.

The robot took the turn and began to travel slowly down the tunnel. The camera pointing straight ahead gave the impression that the tunnel went down a gradual incline.

Then all of sudden the robot began to show evidence of self destruction. Right there in the tunnel, it seemed to begin to melt. The picture continued to transfer an image but it was obvious that the robot had broken down and was disintegrating. It didn't instantly disappear, but it was slowly melting.

"Well, I was hoping something like that wouldn't happen. The Dean will not be very happy when I tell him that the robot is gone. This baby cost General Electric 3.7 million dollars to construct and field test."

"Ouch. But, how could that have happened?" Brooke asked.

"Apparently the robot came in contact with a substance

that causes metal to dissolve. Perhaps some acid-like molecules that exist in gaseous form."

"At least we've got the video to study," Luciano said.

"Yes, that has been salvaged," the Professor replied. "Hopefully you and Luciano learned something from that very expensive trip."

"We most certainly did. The vision of the human ghost, if that is what it was, the rapidly aging girl, and the tunnel to the right, plus the acidity in the region, which destroyed the robot. All of that plus the images on tape are valuable to our research."

Larry Ball and the students were told to come up to the conference room to view the tape.

"We'll need to see that the robot is safely brought up into the truck," Larry said.

"Not necessary. We've lost it."

"Lost it? Like it ran wild?"

"No, like it disintegrated. Sort of melted into a pile of 3.7 million dollars of ashes."

"Oh, my goodness. We'll be up soon."

Chapter Twenty-One

Everyone was debriefed of what was done and what happened to the robot. Larry and the students were anxious to see the tape and so it was rewound and played for the six to study.

"Let me warn you, you're going to see quite a gruesome figure once the robot enters the tunnel," Brooke cautioned. "Then you're going to see a teenage girl, and as she goes farther into the tunnel she will age significantly. Finally, the robot turns down a tunnel to the right and as it looks down a gradual slope, it begins to melt."

The six watched. Since the three were briefed, there were no surprised expressions or comments—just six people intently looking at what no human eyes had seen before.

It was Larry who spoke up when the teenage girl appeared and then seemed to age the farther she went into the tunnel. "I didn't recognize the girl, but as she ages, I can tell that the woman looks like Carolyn Spiker who went into the Triangle looking for Father Jim and Reverend Hogan. Then, she gets much older, so it is only when she appears about age 50 that she looks like Carolyn.

"I think the first ghost was Chip Hogan. It appears that once you go that far into the tunnel, you have gone about as far as you can go without losing your humanness completely. My guess is that if he were to head toward the opening in the Triangle he would be back to his earthly age."

"Really?" Brooke said.

"Well, you guys are the experts, I'm just prognosticating based on my thinking that I saw Carolyn Spiker there for a split second."

Others looked to Luciano for a supportive nod or a comment. He only sat and stared at the monitor and appeared to be in deep thought.

"OK, here goes Casper down the incline and soon it will simply begin to melt, for lack of a better word," the Professor said.

"Yes, there it goes. Oh, what a loss," one of the students said.

Brooke's cell phone rang. She rose from her chair and walked away from the group.

"Hello."

"Miss Parmore, this is the Sheriff."

"Yes, Sheriff. What can I do for you?"

"Well, it's really what I can do for you."

"OK, what do you have for me?"

"I got a call from the Constable in Sudbury. He's got the strangest case he's ever seen. He's really at a loss."

"How's that?"

"He called the nursing home where Dr. Sister was a resident. The attendant said she went to his room to check on him and when she got there all she saw were three piles of clothes and a small dust pile. The attendant said that one pile of clothes belonged to Dr. Sister, but she can't identify the others."

"Was one a polka dot dress?"

"Yes, as a matter of fact it was."

"Winnie was wearing a polka dot dress this morning when we called on her."

"That's what I've got."

"Well, needless to say, that's very interesting," Brooke said, writing down the information. "I will report to Dr. DiNatale and see how he responds. Guess there's no trip to Sudbury in my future."

"No, I guess not."

"Thanks, Sheriff."

"Sure, Miss Parmore."

"What's the news?" Luciano asked.

"The attendant in the nursing home up in Sudbury said she found three piles of clothes on the floor of his room and under each pile of clothes was a small dust pile."

"Hmmm, just like the research I was referring to a day or so ago."

"Yes, that's right."

"How did Winnie and Bea get there? In a private jet?" Luciano asked.

"Good question. I can see that they could 'arrive' there as spirits, but how did the polka dot dress get there?" Brooke asked.

"That is one to stump me, Brooke. I can see spirit transference, but I can't see a transference of clothes."

"Maybe it wasn't the same polka dot dress Winnie was wearing this morning?" Luciano asked.

"It had to be. The old man doesn't have a few polka dot dresses in his drawer for when Winnie and Bea visit," Brooke said, humorously.

"Oh, now I wouldn't jump to conclusions here," Luciano replied. "You are constantly looking at things of the spirit with eyes and a brain from the physical world. The two do not make good bedfellows, Brooke. Common sense and paradigms really must be cast aside. You need to look at all of these happenings with an open mind."

"You're right, Luciano. Listen, did that research paper indicate that these people ever renewed themselves and came back into their clothes?"

"No. Once they were gone, they were gone."

"You may have the next chapter because I have a feeling that they are going to pop up into their clothes when it is convenient or safe to do so."

"Really?"

"Luciano, this mystery has every imaginable twist and crazy thing happening. I don't discount anything."

"Well, have your thoughts, but I'm fairly certain that Bea, Winnie and Dr. Sister have left this earth," Luciano concluded. "My guess is that their only existence is in spirit."

Ghostly LINKS

❦

The professor and his students were about to leave thinking the experiment a failure as far as the robot was concerned. To go home without a 3.7 million dollar piece of technology was a bit troublesome.

Larry turned to look out the window and down the 9th fairway when he said with excitement, "Well, for cryin' out loud. Look at that!"

"What, Larry?" Brooke responded.

"Look out there on the 9th fairway, that's Lucky pulling the robot."

"No way!" Brooke said, looking toward the window.

"Well, take a look for yourself."

"Oh, my gosh, it is!" Brooke ran to the door. "Lucky!! What did you find, boy?"

Lucky released his hold on the robot and came running to greet his master. He jumped up on Brooke with his tail wagging and his tongue hanging out as he panted in excitement to see her.

"What is going on?" Professor Divotski said. "Now we have robots appearing as ghosts? I'm going to go crazy before this thing is solved. Am I seeing things or is that our melted robot out there on the fairway?"

"That's our robot, no question about that," one of his graduate students said.

"But how can it be?"

"Well, I suspect the same thing that happens to people happened to that piece of machine," Luciano said.

"What's that mean?" Brooke asked.

"A person apparently goes in and ages like Carolyn did and as he, or she, comes out, he regains his age in life years on this planet. So, the robot went in a "young" robot; and then as it went farther into the tunnel, it simply grew old, so to speak, and melted down, its way of aging.

"Lucky knew somehow that this robot was important to Brooke, so Lucky went in and pulled the robot out. As it got closer and closer to the golf course, it became young again. But, it didn't have the power from our control device, because we thought it a mass of molten metal. Lucky had to drag it out; and like a stick thrown to a dog, he tried to bring it back to his master, Brooke."

"Well, I'll be," the professor said, shaking his head in disbelief. "I've seen it all now."

"Let's see if the radio control works," the professor said, as he went to the joy stick and turned on the power. When he directed the robot to move it did and so he brought it up to the pro shop while everyone stood in awe and gave it a round of applause, as if Casper had just finished a community 5K race.

"People, and in this case a dog, are pulled into the tunnel for some reason and by some power," Luciano reasoned. "We saw Carolyn there; a very old man that we think might be Chip, and now Lucky. Maybe the Triangle has some power to attract people, select people I would imagine, to its tunnel."

"Yes, but there has to be something at the core of the tunnel that we haven't seen yet," Brooke said. "I have a feeling we've only touched the surface of this fascinating plot of land."

"I agree," Luciano replied.

"Do you need Casper anymore, Miss Parmore, or may we go back to the university for an analysis?" the professor asked, much relieved to have his multimillion dollar robot back in good shape.

"Now that the robot's functional once again, I think our plan was to send Casper back in after dark so we see if we can discover anything under the cover of darkness. Yes, that was the plan. So, you want it going back to work tonight?"

"Yes, I think so. Do you agree, Luciano?"

"Yes, definitely. If you don't mind, I suggest we set Casper in the Triangle and not go into the tunnel. I'm very curious what is to be found when we can look around a larger segment of the Triangle."

"OK, the students and I will be back about 9:30, if that's okay with you."

"Yes, I think Casper can enter about ten or so. I think about an hour max would give us quite a bit of information."

"Fine. We'll put the robot in our truck and be back later."

"Great. Thanks, Professor," Brooke said.

Larry went into the kitchen and found a fine steak for Lucky to enjoy. It was payment for a well-deserved late afternoon of work.

"You know it was chance that I brought Lucky with me today," Brooke said. "I don't like to leave him alone, but I had a feeling that Lucky would have some role to play."

"No way, now you are predicting the future?" Luciano said in jest. "Have you been in the Triangle, Miss Parmore?"

"Are you kidding me? You couldn't get me in that Triangle for all the tea in China," Brooke said, shaking her head.

"What's Bea doing in China," Luciano said with a hearty laugh.

"You can laugh all you want, but that little misunderstanding by Winnie was a major, major clue today. You do realize what she admitted to today, don't you?"

"Well, yes, that something happened in the hospital involving the woman introduced to us as Bea."

"No, as I told you, I think she thought you said 'making Bea' and she panicked because she realized that you had figured out that she had made Bea."

"Literally made Bea?" Luciano asked.

"That's what I think."

"And what do you mean, 'made Bea'?"

"I think she was created in a laboratory," Brooke reasoned.

"You mean mad passionate love was made between Winnie and Doc Sister, so that Bea was conceived in a hospital lab, or do you mean Winnie put a collection of organs together to literally make Bea, or maybe Winnie just wished for a daughter and she appeared, as if made in the laboratory."

"Of those three, the latter."

"You've got a point, Brooke. But, let me remind you that this is back in time, tens of years ago, when medical techniques for this were unheard of."

"After the last few days you actually can believe that nothing is impossible, Luciano? Give me a break. What is there left for the imagination, anyway?" Brooke asked.

"Oh, you'd be surprised. You should take one of my classes."

"After this investigation, I could co-teach the class with you."

"Well, maybe she did make Bea, and if she did, she did a good job of it. I was being honest whether she heard tea or Bea."

"And, now we learn that the three of them can go from a material and physical set of beings to nothing, even leaving behind clothes and their earthly minerals."

"Yeah, pretty amazing isn't it?" Luciano asked.

"Was it spontaneous combustion, Luciano?"

"No, I don't think so. I think it was simply a case of shedding the clothes and going directly to the spirit world."

"Simply?" Brooke asked. "I've never even heard of this before and you talk about it like it is some common occurrence."

"Well, it is a lot more common than you think, even though the average citizen has never heard of such a thing."

Chapter Twenty-Two

Brooke, Luciano and Larry chose to get a bite to eat at a local restaurant. They didn't want a large and fancy meal, but only wished for something light. To get their mind off of the Triangle they talked about things of general interest. Nobody paid much attention to what each other said, as the conversation was meant to be frivolous, so that their minds could take a break from all the craziness that consumed them.

They returned to the Ghostly Links Country Club and wondered how best to spend the time before Casper would return for a second foray into the Triangle.

Right when Brooke thought she would have a few hours to relax, her cell phone rang.

"Hello."

"I'm trying to reach Brooke Parmore, an investigator looking into the mystery at Ghostly Links."

"I am Brooke Parmore. Can I help you?"

"Yes, I think so. I didn't want to share some information for the longest time, but I'm at a point where I must talk to somebody about what's happening or I'll go crazy."

"That's fine. I'd love to talk with you. Shall we plan a breakfast meeting?"

"That would fine, but I don't need much time really. If I could see you anytime this evening, I would be very grateful."

"Sure. As a matter of fact, I have an hour or two right now."

"Where can we meet?"

"Can I invite my colleague to listen?"

"That's fine. I don't care who listens. I've simply got to unload all of this."

"Can you come to the Ghostly Links Golf Course?"

"Yes. I know where that is, Lord knows I know."

"We'll be in the conference room of the clubhouse. When can we expect you?"

"Well, on the physical plane of time and space limitations it will take me quite awhile. In spirit, a snap of human fingers."

"Your choice, I suppose," Brooke said. "You mean, you can appear right here when you hang up?"

"Yes, or even as we continue to talk."

"Let me brief my colleague that you will be joining us. Give me a minute or two to do that and then we'll await your arrival."

"Fine. See you in a couple of minutes."

"Yes. Thank you for calling."

"You're welcome."

"Luciano and Larry. Listen to this. That caller wants to talk to us and he is going to transform himself from spirit to a human and appear right in this room in about a minute or two."

"Well, that ought to be something to see," Larry said. "Who will appear?"

"I don't know. I forgot to ask for a name."

"A man or a woman? Not that it matters," Luciano asked.

"I don't know how the spirit will manifest itself but the caller sounded like a male voice. Ironically, the voice sounded a bit familiar, but I can't place where I may have heard it. This should be an interesting interview. The person said that he had to talk to me and really seemed as if waiting until morning would be too late."

"Too late for what?" Larry asked.

"I don't know."

Then without any noise or air disturbance, the form of a man began to materialize in the room. It wasn't instant; it was more like watching a film develop. First, within about thirty seconds they saw the form of a person develop, and then in another ten seconds this form seemed to go from a trance-like state to a fully functioning human being.

"Good evening," the spirit-turned-human said.

"Father McDuffy! Oh, my God, it's so good to see you again!" Brooke exclaimed as she stepped forward to give him a hug.

"Likewise, Brooke. It's nice to see you as well."

"Father, this is Larry Ball, the pro here. Oh, wait a minute. You know Larry! Of course, you play out here in your league."

"Yes, I know Larry. Good to see you again," Father Jim said, while stepping forward to shake Larry's hand.

"Father Jim. Good to see you. Ready for nine holes?"

"Not until I correct my horrendous slice, Larry."

"This is my colleague, Luciano DiNatale. He is from the Center for Extracelestial Studies in New Jersey and is a world-renowned expert on the paranormal."

"Nice to meet you, Luciano."

"The pleasure is mine, Father."

"Well, thanks for your call. You have something to share with us?" Brooke asked.

"Yes, I do. I feel like one of my parishioners coming into the Confessional."

"Oh, my goodness, that's a change of roles. Do you want Larry to leave?" Brooke said with a smile, recalling the many times she had sat before him to confess her sins.

"No, what I've got to say can be heard by anyone. I wanted you, Brooke, to hear it because I think it will help you with your work and perhaps Luciano already knows what I will say since he's an expert in the paranormal."

"Oh, not a good assumption, Father. I'm learning everyday."

"I guess I should begin at the beginning. I did go into the Triangle of my own choosing. Chip challenged my faith as I recall and my human memory tells me that I did not see anything out of the ordinary in the Triangle. It looked like any other densely wooded, marshy, area. It wasn't until I fled the Triangle that I realized that a transformation had occurred."

"Excuse me for interrupting, but did Chip come out?"

"I don't think so. I say that because I do not recall ever seeing him in human form after that day."

"But you see him in spirit form?" Brooke asked.

"Oh, yes. At will. I like him. He likes my jokes and we all like those who like our jokes, correct?"

"I suppose so."

"Anyway, while in human form and out in Connecticut at the retreat, I ... let me digress a moment and say that one of the benefits of living a dual existence is being able to pick and choose the plane and how it best fits into what you want to do or have happen."

"Explain, please."

"Well, take the Bishop sending me to Connecticut for example. When I want to be there in human form, I am, but when I don't want to be there, I simply go to my spirit form."

"Sort of like selecting your state of being, right, Father?" Luciano asked.

"Yes, you can do it too, you just don't think you can, but I'm getting ahead of myself here.

"As I was saying, out in Connecticut, and in human form, I decided to have a physical. There is a history of skin cancer in my family, so I try to get regular checkups. I went to a doctor who was recommended by the director of the retreat center. The doctor said I appeared to be cancer free and quite healthy for my age, but he was intrigued by what he thought was a sebaceous cyst in my back. He said to simply keep an eye on it, which is impossible since I have no way of seeing the middle of my back, but he meant it figuratively. He said to come back in a few weeks and if it had grown he would take a biopsy or remove it, but if it was not uncomfortable, he'd leave it alone.

"A few weeks went by. I went back to the doc and he said it appeared to be the same but when he felt it and massaged it a bit, he said it wasn't a cyst as it was too hard. He thought it needed to be looked at. So, with my permission he deadened the area and started to take it out, but it wouldn't come out. He couldn't cut the connector and so he simply washed it in antiseptic and put it back.

"He couldn't explain what it was or why it was there. Nor could I except that I had gone into the Triangle and had the ability to live in human form or in spirit form. Oh, by the way, he referred to it as, 'The Chip.'"

"Let me interrupt because it is on my mind and I don't want to lose the thought," Brooke said.

"Sure, go ahead."

"I hope I am not breaking confidence but we've heard of some of your activity on the spirit level."

"Oh, my gosh, then I guess I truly am in the Confessional. Wait till I get on my knees." All four smiled and chuckled. Father Jim's humor was alive and well.

"We've learned that you would appear in the convent and tell the nuns your jokes," Brooke said.

"Oh, my, my sins in the spirit life come to haunt me on the physical plane."

"Hardly a sin, Father."

"Well, you didn't hear the half of it. My wish was to be in one of the convents for awhile. I was always so curious about that place. I mean, wouldn't you be? I was always wondering what they talked about, what they did, and did they really live this angelic life? I knew we priests didn't, being human and all, but I always wished I could be in the convent sort of as a mouse in the corner.

"So, yes, I was there and in many others as well. I'd tell my jokes and they would all blush and laugh. I felt like I brought them to the comedy club, and you know what, they seemed to really enjoy them. Well, not all of them, the prudish didn't like them, but the majority seemed to clamor for more."

"I'll bet you were a breath of fresh air." Luciano said.

"Well, I don't know about fresh air, but my wish was finally granted and you know what, stupid wish, because it was all quite boring once I got in there. They are holy women, no question about it, but they just work, pray, eat, sleep and repeat this cycle everyday. I soon realized that I should have wished for a month in Miami at the Doral Country Club playing 36 holes of golf a day and enjoying the warm sun. But, we all have choices to make."

"Ghostly Links isn't good or challenging enough for you, Father?" Larry said with a chuckle.

"Not good enough in February, Larry. Otherwise your rough takes my slice as well as the next course. After awhile they all look alike; I know I've played hundreds of them.

"Anyway, I seem to get off my topic. The reason I wanted to speak with you, Brooke, is to tell you that I believe you should stop your investigation into the Triangle."

"Really?"

"Yes. I think it best to leave well enough alone so to speak. The Triangle has been there for decades, life has gone along in predictable fashion. People are satisfied with their choices. Larry has warning signs posted along the Triangle and the golfers sign a release form. People take risks all the time and this is one more risk.

"The more you and Luciano look into this, the more disruption will occur. I've seen so much of it already and there will be much more."

"Can you give us an example, Father?" Luciano asked.

"Bea and Winnie and Dr. Sister were living, as I live, in two worlds so to speak. I mean it is all the same "world," but to you, they are in two different worlds. They were happy in their existence, and then they felt it best to abandon the physical existence because Winnie misunderstood Luciano's comment which wouldn't have happened if you two were not investigating this thing.

"Bob Rule has shared information with you. He has told me he regrets it because he told you information in great confidence and you told Luciano what he told you. Being human always causes a breakdown in some way of promises; it's just the nature of a human being."

Brooke glanced down at the floor feeling guilty for sharing what Bob Rule had told her after saying she would tell no one and to trust her.

"I could go on and on," Father Jim continued, "but, suffice it to say, it would be better, in my opinion, to simply bring this investigation to a close and let everyone, in physical form and spirit form, return to the lives that are comfortable for all."

"But it needs to be explained, Father," Brooke said. "People need to know."

"I disagree, they don't need to know. It is only the curious aspect of the human psychic that causes people to wonder, to spend time gossiping, sharing what they know. Everybody was getting along just fine before Cliff walked in to find his ball and everybody would get along fine if you folks just closed shop and allowed all to return to normal, because if you don't, the chip will be activated."

"The chip will be activated?" Brooke said, confused.

"Yes. The chip has a call home feature. And, all of us fear it."

"A call home feature?" Luciano asked.

"Out of our control is the call home feature and if it is activated, all of us with chips will be called home like salmon returning to their spawning grounds. Actually if the chip could be analyzed it would be discovered that the homing feature of the salmon is the same that exists in our chip. "

"Who controls the chip, Father?" Brooke asked.

"I hope my answering that question will not cause activation."

"Well, don't answer if you think it will."

"I take the risk, because I really would like you folks to stop the investigation. The chip is controlled by Doctor Sister."

"That's what I thought you would say," Luciano said. "The experiments at the hospital, right Father? He perfected something at the hospital, didn't he?"

"Yes, he did."

"He controls all of you from a nursing home in Sudbury, Ontario?" Brooke said, feeling she is answering some of the mystery.

"Well, that's where he goes for care in his human form which, by the way, will continue to live forever. He will never die in his human form. And, I wouldn't say he controls all of us as much as to say, he can activate the chips if he chooses and that can be anytime in your concept of time."

"He will never die?"

"That's right and actually you never die either, but ..."

"Wait a minute, we never die?" Brooke asked.

"It's an illusion created by the limitations of your senses."

"We never die?" Brooke asked again, astounded.

"Of course not, you sort of lose your skin like a snake. I guess that's the best way to describe it, but humans just think they die, when in reality, they simply move to a spirit form."

"Simply?"

"Actually, yes. It is quite a simple thing. You'll see when your time comes."

"This is why some people say they don't fear death?" Luciano asked.

"I suppose so. I mean, I feared it when I was perceiving myself to be only human. Why wouldn't we fear it, it is all we know and we don't want to lose what we think is all that there is. But, the physical plane isn't really all that cool, if I may use the vernacular. I mean it's OK, but it is only a glimpse into the beauty and the potential for joy that is in the spirit life."

"Is there a Heaven, Father?" Brooke asked.

"Oh, yes, most assuredly. But, you can experience it on earth just as you can on the spirit level." Larry glanced over at Brooke and their eyes met.

"Then I suppose there is also a hell?" Luciano asked.

"Oh, yes. It's disharmony, low frequency, conflicts just as you experience them on the human side. We wouldn't call it hell or heaven on the spirit side, but there are degrees of tuning into higher and higher frequencies. You see, on the human plane everything except God, your word by the way for the highest frequency, is as the Chinese say, 'Ying-yang.' That is to say, everything has an opposite, because it is only by having opposites that you can understand a concept. Hot only has meaning if you have cold, up only has meaning if you have a down and I could go for thousands of words in your lexicon. But, on the spirit side there are no concepts of opposites. Very nice by the way."

"Back to your request, Father," Brooke said. "We have a need to know what this is all about. We can't have people giving into their curiosity, inability to read, or dares, or whatever motivation and having their lives ruined. It isn't our way of doing this on this side as you know."

"But, that's the problem. Lives are not bcing ruined."

"Tell that to Jane Hooker, if you don't agree with me," Brooke said.

"Jane has choices like everyone, but Cliff's life is not being ruined, I can assure you of that."

"You mean now that he has a Catholic connection?"

Father Jim laughed out loud. "Oh, yes, our friendly game. Cliff and I have a ball with all of that. He gets a big kick out of having a Catholic priest for a friend and I certainly enjoy having a member of the Jehovah's Witnesses to josh with."

"Has he become a Catholic?" Brooke asked.

"Goodness no. On the spirit side, you don't have all of these groupings. You simply are in tune so to speak. On the physical plane, he chooses to be a member of a church, and that's fine. We, at least you, Brooke, and I, choose Catholicism and we live with that faith, just as our friends in all other denominations do, or even those without a denomination make a choice. Cliff can't convert to anything on the spirit side because there is no group to convert to. He can raise his frequency and he's working on that as am I."

"But the Crucifix on his living room wall?" Brooke said.

"Oh, yes, the Crucifix. Just one of my jokes, I guess."

"Jane doesn't think it is very funny."

"Yes, Cliff made it clear to me. I will change my ways with Cliff and Jane. It is hard to predict humor."

"Back to your request. We keep getting off target but this is all so fascinating. Did Dr. Sister ask, or tell you, to come and meet with us?" Brooke asked.

"No. When we are on the physical plane we have free will, as do you, and I thought there's no good coming from all of your work, so I thought I'd ask you to consider stopping it."

"It's gone crazy, Father," Larry said. "You probably wouldn't be shocked knowing human nature as you do, but we've got bus tours wanting to come here; I've gotten calls from popular TV show hosts, *Oprah* and even *Maury Povish*. I've heard all kinds of intervention theories and researchers wanting to conduct experiments. I think, if Brooke calls it off, we'll have her replaced with some nut that will really screw things up. At least with Brooke and Luciano we know we've got sincere and professional people trying to make sense of this."

"Thank you, Larry, and I think that once it can all be explained, things will die down," Brooke said.

"No, they won't, Brooke. Once they can be explained, everyone will want to enter the Triangle. We'll have mass hysteria."

"Why would everyone want to enter?" Luciano asked.

"Well, you've taken me to the point where I will have to give away the secret of the Triangle. I am only doing this so you will see why you must stop this investigation lest word gets out and invokes total hysteria and chaos."

Father Jim took a deep breath and continued, "When people enter the Triangle, they are told instantly, within a second of crossing the imaginary barrier, that they can have a wish granted, any wish, and that a chip will be implanted, that if activated, will call them home. These people or even those who simply break the barrier by reaching in, are brought into the tunnel where this transformation takes place. They, if they choose, are led back outside the Triangle on solid ground. This all happens before someone outside the Triangle can see a change in the person. And, the human mind cannot record what is happening."

"So, any wish is granted?" Luciano concluded.

"Yes it is."

"Cliff's heart?"

"He didn't want a bad heart. I don't think a woman named Lucy Putterbee came to talk to you. But, she's been in and she wanted to play the piano. She can now. Her first trip in was a wish for only the ability to play with her right hand, thus she needed a trip back for the second hand."

"Does it matter what you wish for?" Brooke asked.

"No, the wish is taken magnetically from the body. You don't verbalize a wish, it is in the subconscious. All thoughts, past and present, are energy and so Dr. Sister simply devised a method to extract the wish energy within the brain."

"How about telling people that this is exactly what happens in the Triangle?" Luciano asked.

"Not a good idea. I say this because it is a lot like getting a medical test to tell you when you will die. Do you really want to know? Do you really want a wish to come true? The old saying, 'Be careful what you wish for, you just might get it,' is true. The effects of the wish cannot be understood when you go to the Triangle. The effects of the wish are the person's responsibility on the physical plane. Sometimes the wish brings happiness and sometimes it brings pain and discomfort. It is similar to people winning the lottery. Some make wise choices and are happy. Others make lousy choices and become miserable."

"So, you think if we told people that entering the Triangle will bring a subconscious wish to reality, many would want to enter, but they could not handle the effects of the granted wish."

"They can handle the effects of the wish, but their choices affect what happens to them. So, you see, it is better to simply stop the investigation, let some time pass and other events will take center stage and this will slowly go away. Then Dr. Sister can return to the nursing home, Winnie and Bea can be at peace, and all who entered the Triangle will live with their wish, the consequences of the wish, and the fear of the call to come home."

Father Jim then added, "The decision is yours. I pray you make the right one. Thank you for listening and hearing my plea."

As easily as Father Jim had appeared, within 30 seconds he was gone.

∞

Brooke, Larry, and Luciano sat in stunned silence in the conference room of the Ghostly Links Country Club. It was as if Father Jim gave his most compelling homily and the parishioners sat in silence to allow the profound message to sink in and to reflect on it in total silence.

Brooke broke the silence with what sounded like a prayer, "God, I don't know what to do. Any thoughts?"

"What Father Jim says is logical and seems to be a solution that would sit well with a lot of folks," Larry said.

"Yes, but I agree with Brooke and what she said earlier," Luciano remarked. "She said that if we don't solve it, tomorrow it will be an issue and on and on. Science wants to solve it and explain it, and put it behind us, so to speak. I say, we go on and finish the investigation."

"I see both sides," Brooke said. "I have a great deal of respect for Father Jim. Behind all of the corny and off-color jokes, is a wise and compassionate soul. His advice makes sense. But, my role in life is to make sense of what is mysterious. People need closure to the mysteries that are all about them. Man is in a continual search for answers to the unknown. If we don't stick with it, we quit, and we can't quit, because we will only shut down until another soul walks into the Triangle and someone talks about it. Then the questions come back and somebody else will look into this."

"I guess I am speaking selfishly," Larry said. "I simply want to get back to managing a golf course, and the sooner the better."

"That's easy enough to understand," Brooke replied sympathetically.

"It sounds like you two think you should proceed and I'm certainly willing to go along with that," Larry said. "I only ask that you solve this thing as soon as possible."

"We will, Larry," Brooke said, assuredly. "Father Jim already answered part of the mystery. People who enter the Triangle have their wish come true, but in receiving this gift, they stand ready for Dr. Sister to activate some homing device that ends their physical existence."

"Yes, that's true, but that's only the tip of the iceberg. We know what happens, but how does it happen?" Luciano asked. "What power has been harnessed so that Dr. Sister can give and take away with the activation of some device?"

"Yes, and the bigger picture is that if Dr. Sister can give wishes and deny people a physical life, what other uses for the power might he have or might he unleash in the future?"

"What are you thinking?" Luciano asked.

"I'm thinking of changing the chip so that instead of giving a wish, he causes the people to serve him and <u>his</u> wish, and only he would know what that wish would be."

"Right, and Father Jim said that he would live forever so the future of mankind could rest with this man."

"That is very scary!!" Brooke said.

Larry said, "I've got an idea."

"What might that be?" Brooke asked.

"How about if we simply build an attractive building all around the Triangle. We would basically seal off the Triangle so people could no longer go in, even if they wanted to. In doing this, we take away curiosity. Who wants to come to a golf course to look at a three-sided concrete structure?"

"You are back wanting to find a quick fix to the issue," Brooke explained. "We've got to get to the core of this."

"Oh, I know, just thought I'd drop that little vision on you guys," Larry said, but then he got serious. "What if we had Casper take in some highly explosive device and detonate it. Maybe a bomb going off would clear the area of all the mystery." Larry couldn't believe what he had just said, knowing that he was sitting on a gold mine with a consultant, planning how to bring him millions.

"That is just another quick fix," Brooke said, shaking her head from side to side. "No, we've somehow got to get to the core. Something, some power, some technology, is at the heart of all of this."

"Yes, there has to be, because the chip is imbedded in each person's physical body," Luciano said.

"The chip has to be made somewhere and it has to be implanted somewhere and by someone - even if it be a ghost," Brooke surmised.

"And, remember, Cliff's heart was removed. Where is the old heart? Who removed it?" Luciano asked. "For all we know, others are walking around without livers, lungs, stomachs, and spleens."

"Right. As Father said, we never heard of Lucy Putterbee and her learning to play the piano. Who knows how many others have snuck out here in the night to explore the Triangle."

"So, I guess we get back to work and although Father Jim would like us to cease our work, we choose to continue," Luciano said, looking for support.

"Yes," Brooke replied. "And, I guess we begin tonight when Casper goes into the Triangle. We'll see if anything can be learned at that time."

Chapter Twenty-Three

Dr. Sister, Winnie and Bea were in spirit form because they feared the consequences of being found on the physical plane.

"I fear that after all these years, we may be discovered and if we are, I fear that the end may be near," Dr. Sister said.

"I think Dr. DiNatale knows that we made Bea, and I know that because that's what he said," Winnie replied. "He thought he was paying me a compliment, but what he did was to let me know that they were on to our experiment."

"Are you sure he complemented you on making Bea?" Dr. Sister asked. "There is absolutely no way anyone on earth could know that. Virtually impossible!"

"All I know is what I heard," Winnie said, assured that she had heard clearly what the man had said.

"Because if he knows that, he knows that the laboratory exists under the hospital, down in the tunnels. He knows about the chips and the process of using them, the aging and youth embellishing process, the frequency field in the Triangle. The frequency is such that no human can experience it, so that is why he can't know that we made Bea. Bea, does this make sense to you?"

"No, because they were investigating the mystery of the Triangle and if the man knew that you two had made me, they would not have come back to ask questions. I mean, why would they ask questions when they already had answers?" Bea asked.

"Precisely!" Dr. Sister replied.

"Do you think we should remove the two from the earth?" Winnie asked.

"We can't control anyone who doesn't have a wish to be fulfilled. You know that," Dr. Sister replied.

"Yes, but they wish to solve this mystery, our mystery," Winnie said. "That is their wish."

"Right, but they have to enter the Triangle of their own free will," Dr. Sister reminded the two.

"Yes, and when they do, they belong to us," Winnie said with a smile.

"No, they will have their wish fulfilled and their wish is to have their case solved," Dr. Sister said.

"True, but once their wish is granted, you activate the homing device and end their earthly lives. Then the mystery remains unsolved and our control continues."

"When I activate the homing device everyone who has ever entered the Triangle will come to it and dissolve. But, if I do that, I lose my immortality because the aliens from the Zolofte Galaxy will not have their one million warriors.

"I think we wait awhile," Dr. Sister replied.

❦

Professor Divotski, Tom and Cheri returned to Ghostly Links with Casper in the back of a university truck. Preparations for Casper to enter the Triangle were begun.

As before, Larry and the two students took the truck to a point in the Triangle and parked it about five yards from the designated entrance. The professor was once again monitoring the controls, making sure all systems were go.

"I think Casper should go into the Triangle while we slowly rotate the camera," Brooke advised. "In doing so, we can see if anything appears in the darkness. Then we can turn on the light and have Casper move around the Triangle area. We'll see if anything interesting appears. Is that acceptable to you, Luciano? How about you, Professor?" Both nodded in agreement.

Twilight became night and all was set for Casper to go into the Triangle. Larry and the students had flashlights to monitor the area so no one would go into the Triangle while Casper was doing its work.

Professor Divotski used the joy stick to move Casper into the Triangle as before. The camera mounted on the top was turned on, but nothing was observed on the television monitor.

"Rotate the camera, please," Brooke requested.

The professor used a switch to allow the camera to pan the area.

"Stop it. Look!" Brooke said.

"Oh, very interesting. Very interesting. Look at that, would you?" Luciano said with excitement.

"Glad we're getting this on tape," Brooke replied. "Some folks are going to be pretty excited to see this."

"Let's just say it's like a scientist seeing a flying saucer on the horizon and being able to verify that it's a flying saucer and not a reflection, or a trick photo," Larry offered as excited as a scientist can get.

"Luciano. That picture alone will make you the most famous paranormal scientist in the world. As if you are not that already."

"Professor, can you zoom in a bit so we can get a better look?" Luciano asked.

"Sure. I can do that." Instantly the zoom lens was activated and Luciano and Brooke were astonished at what was before their eyes. It was simply amazing.

"If we had taken Father McDuffy's advice, we would never have seen something like this," Brooke said.

"You're right. Absolutely awesome."

"OK, Professor. Can you now have Casper move around within the Triangle?" Brooke asked. "Please go back to the wide-angle lens so we can look around. Leave the light off. I want it very dark."

"OK, here we go, I'm moving him to the apex out by the 8th green and the 9th tee."

On the screen appeared hundreds and probably thousands of ghosts, huddled and floating off the ground. It's hard to explain what they saw, but the color was sort of a dim glow.

They could see the forms of the beings, but they had to use their imagination to see a human form.

There were no legs but there were arms that seemed to move back and forth like someone in a swimming pool up to their waist and skimming across the water going from left to right. There were heads, but no hair or sense organs, or at least none that the three could see. They seemed to be doing nothing and they didn't seem disturbed by Casper or any noise that its mechanical parts were making.

"OK, now turn on the light and let's see what they do," Brooke said.

The professor turned on the light and all that happened was that the light masked the images on the screen.

"Turn the light off, please." The professor did as he was asked.

"OK, please zoom in on one so we can get a better look," Luciano asked. When the image they zoomed in on was enlarged they could see that the ghost was obviously transparent. The color was more of a light grey than white. The size of the ghost was like a small adult.

All of a sudden, two or three ghosts, it was hard to tell, moved quickly to the side. "Follow them with the camera, if you can," Brooke demanded.

The ghosts actually left the Triangle. Casper moved to the edge of the Triangle and the camera was able to catch the ghosts among Larry and the students. They seemed to intermingle with the physical beings.

Brooke picked up her walkie-talkie. "Larry, Larry. Come in."

"Yes, Brooke. Successful trip for Casper?"

"Yes, most definitely. Do you sense a ghost in your presence?"

"No, should I?"

"Yes, you should. There are two or three around you, Tom, and Cheri."

"Hmm, guess my eyes don't have the capability of picking up their auras."

"If it weren't for the lens on the camera that can detect an energized form that the eye can't see, we wouldn't see them either."

"If I reach out, would I touch one?"

"One is standing, or I should say, positioned right in front of you. This being appears to want to shake your hand."

Larry reached out and moved his hand. Brooke could see him moving his hand right through the grey matter. But, Larry did not sense anything.

The ghosts left the three and floated away, moving out onto the golf course. Their presence, which Brooke took to be continuous, certainly gave meaning to the name of the club, Ghostly Links.

Since the decision had been made not to have Casper go into a tunnel on this trip, Brooke and Luciano felt that the mission was successful. The professor was asked to bring Casper out of the Triangle and to guide it onto the truck. Larry and the students drove back to the clubhouse. The three came in and so did Lucky, who had been patiently waiting outside for Brooke to finish her work and take him home to a meal and a good sleep.

Larry and the students were anxious to see the videotape. "Well, what have we got to look forward to?" Tom asked.

"Pretty exciting, actually," Professor Divotski replied.

"Let her roll. Ready, Larry?"

"Yup, I want to meet my new friend, the ghost that wanted to shake my hand."

The professor began the video and the six watched with rapt attention.

"Whoa," said Larry, when the first image appeared on the screen. "Boy, is that a sight."

"I thought you'd be surprised at that," Brooke said.

"Boy, oh, boy, you can say that again. I never would have thought something like that would be in this triangular plot of land. Amazing, simply amazing."

"OK, now here are some of your friends as Casper moves about inside the Triangle," Brooke said.

"Oh my, they look like a happy crew. Wonder if any of my members are in that group?" Larry said, with a smile.

"OK, now watch them, a few of them leave the Triangle and gather around the three of you."

"You know around that time, I felt a pull to enter the Triangle," said Cheri.

"Really, tell us about that," Luciano said.

"I felt drawn, yes, that's it. I felt drawn to the Triangle."

"Would you have gone in?" Brooke asked.

"No, I don't think I would, but I'm just saying that I entertained the thought that I might like to go in, and it happened right then when those ghosts were around us."

"Hmmm, interesting. Did you feel that way, Tom?" Luciano asked.

"No. I was getting a little bored and I recall thinking, I'm ready to end this. All we're doing is standing outside waiting for Casper to do his work."

"How about you, Larry. I know you were talking to me on the walkie-talkie, but did you sense anything?"

"Nope. That one ghost seems to have taken a liking to me. Seemed to pick me out and levitate right in front of me, like checking me out."

"Must be that magnetism, huh, Larry?" Brooke said, giving him a smile and a wink. Larry returned it with a nod.

"We'll leave this tape with you. I assume you want it for review and study?" Professor Divotski asked.

"Yes, definitely. Thank you," Brooke replied. "We appreciate all three of you coming out tonight and helping us."

"You're welcome. Call me if Casper can help you in any other way. OK?"

"Sure."

The professor and students left with Casper in the back of the university truck. Casper would go to the lab for a very thorough debriefing.

Brooke took Luciano to his hotel. On her way home, she thought for a second, and decided to say goodnight to Larry in the way he liked to hear, "Good night."

❦

As Brooke and Larry relaxed in the glow of candlelight, their conversation drifted back to the evening visit of Casper to the Triangle.

"What did you think of that first image?" Brooke asked.

"You two are doing the investigation. I can't be sure. You tell me if I am wrong, but we were looking at Dr. Sister, Winnie, and Bea weren't we?"

"Yes, Larry. It was them. At least it was Winnie and Bea. I can only assume the man was Dr. Sister."

"It had to be him. I didn't expect Dr. Sister to be that tall," Larry said. "He looked to be almost seven foot tall."

"It was downright eerie, wasn't it?" Brooke asked, shuddering. "I mean seeing these three glowing and staring back at you without knowing they are staring at anyone. They looked somewhat luminescent, like they were filled with neon gas. Especially, when their heads sort of glowed."

"That's because the concentration of energy is located in the head. It gives off this astral glow. Didn't you think it weird that Bea didn't have any legs or feet?" Larry asked.

"I didn't notice that. I was checking out how tall Dr. Sister was, I guess. She didn't have legs or feet, huh? How do you explain that?"

"I can't explain it. She had legs and feet this morning at her home. I mean she walked around."

Chapter Twenty-Four

Thursday, September 1, 2005

The day began with a light rain. The grass, flowers and farm crops needed it, having gone for a few days with dry heat. The golf course was deserted except for a few of the heartiest players.

Larry planned to attack his desk with its ever growing mountain of mail and phone calls to be returned. Even though Brooke was in his life in a way he never could have imagined a couple of weeks ago, and even though he was juggling a media circus around the Triangle, the work of a golf course professional and manager remained constant. He hoped for a rather quick conclusion to the investigation, a press conference to explain it all and then a gradual return to normalcy.

Brooke was up and, with a golf umbrella for extra protection, took Lucky for a long walk. During the walk, she tried to focus her attention on how best to solve this mysterious case.

Luciano was having breakfast in the hotel coffee shop. He looked out the window to see the misty rain and realized he had not thought to bring an umbrella on this trip.

Brooke thought that the key to solving this mystery was to get into the tunnels. Something had to be there. The old song,

"The bear went over the mountain to see what he could see," was beckoning and now all she had to do was figure out what protection would be needed to go through the tunnels.

Brooke knew that she couldn't walk in; she knew what had happened to Casper when it moved into the cavernous tunnel. *So, what protection could she find that would allow her to live and yet be free from the powerful effects of the forces inside the tunnels?* Brooke thought.

As Luciano was skimming *USA Today*, he too was thinking of tunnel travel. He was thinking that if he knew the tunnel network, they could go down into it by digging from some spot on the golf course. And, once pierced, perhaps some device could be used to explore the tunnels.

Brooke picked Luciano up at the hotel about eight-thirty. On the way to the golf course, they discussed what they had been thinking. Luciano was set on finding any blueprints for the hospital grounds. Brooke would be calling NASA to see if they had any protective suits that could be used if Casper or a human wished to travel in the tunnels.

"You know, this tunnel power has to be activated in some way," Brooke said, staring through the rhythmic back and forth movement of her windshield wipers. "How could Lucky have gotten Casper out of the tunnel? How could he have pulled what appeared to be a molten mass outside as it reassembled itself? How could the doctor safely go through the tunnels without succumbing to the force? How could patients be brought to the county jail cell without some damage to their bodies?"

"I think there must be some master control center. There has to be," Luciano concluded. "Dr. Sister has to control all of this from a central point. But, where is the central point? That's the mystery."

"I think you're right," Brooke said, as they continued their ride to the Country Club.

"So, how to traverse the tunnels safely to discover the command center?" Luciano asked. "That's a major question."

"Yes."

Luciano suggested that Brooke take him to the County Building. He had research to do relative to the tunnel pattern under the golf course. Brooke expected to remain at the golf course, so she loaned him her car and gave him directions to the County Building.

Brooke called NASA from the Country Club. She explained her reason for calling and the operator decided to put her through to Philip Nicklaus. Philip listened to her interesting conundrum and asked if there was any way she could come to their field office in Memphis to talk with a set of people who might be able to help.

"I'll be there this afternoon. Is that possible?"

"Yes, we can see you about one o'clock. Is that okay? Plan to have a late lunch at our center."

"Yes, and thank you very much."

"Be sure to bring those videotapes and anything else you think would help us understand your circumstances."

"Will do. Do you have a runway for corporate jets to land at your facility or must I use the Memphis airport?"

"If we know you're coming, you can land at our airfield."

"Wonderful. I have to call and make arrangements, but I am hoping to find a corporate jet that can bring me there. I'll call you back, Mr. Nicklaus, once my plans are set."

"Fine, I look forward to hearing from you."

Brooke hung up the phone and immediately called Bob Rule in Chicago. "Mr. Rule, I have two reasons for my call. The first is to apologize for breaking your confidence. I guess I thought I would be free to discuss what you told me with Dr. DiNatale. He's working with me on this case and we must share information to successfully solve the mystery."

"I understand and it was the risk I took in telling you. I had hoped what I had shared would remain only with you, but I didn't make it clear I suppose, because I do believe that if I asked you to not even share with your investigator colleague that you would have honored my request. Besides, I am human too, most of the time, and how could I not forgive a woman interested in unlocking the mystery of the Triangle. I accept your apology."

"Thank you. I feel much better," Brooke said, relieved that Bob seemed to understand.

"What is the second reason for your call?"

"I need to be in Memphis by one o'clock this afternoon. I realize this is a bit presumptuous to even be asking, but can you help me?"

"Yes. My pilot, my assistant, and I will be at your airport in about an hour."

"Thank you very much, Bob."

"My pleasure."

Brooke walked into the Pro Shop, greeted Larry, and explained that she'd be going to Memphis and would he please take care of Lucky until she returned, hopefully, in the early evening.

The plane did arrive and was able to land in the misty rain that continued to fall. The door opened on the tarmac and Brooke got on. She was greeted warmly by Bob Rule, the door closed, and the jet began its slow trip to the runway's end for a quick takeoff.

"It is good to see you again, Brooke."

"Likewise, Bob. I can't thank you enough for helping me."

"Would you like a drink or some coffee?"

"Some coffee would be fine, thank you."

Miss Pepper rose and poured a hot cup of coffee for Brooke. Bob was receiving a fax message and simultaneously talking on another phone. He finished his work while Brooke sipped her coffee and spread out some papers of her own.

"Please forgive me, Brooke, work goes on and things must be attended to."

"Oh, I fully understand. Do what you need to do. I'm just so thankful for your help. I think talking to the folks at NASA is key to solving the mystery."

"Yes, tell me what this is all about."

"I have a meeting with Mr. Philip Nicklaus and some others at a NASA field office this afternoon at 1:00. I am hopeful he can tell us some way to travel through the tunnels without coming under the influence of the powers in the Triangle. I thought that if anybody had the technology for this it would be NASA, having to outfit astronauts for travel in foreign environments."

"Yes, I think you're going to the right place. Thanks for inviting me to go along."

"Certainly. It's the least I can do."

"Are you making any progress in understanding the Triangle, Brooke?"

"I am beginning to believe that a doctor who used to work at the mental hospital conducted experiments on patients. He perfected a means to grant people their wish, but with a price. He apparently invented a homing activation switch that will end the earthly existence of all who have entered the Triangle. We are close to solving and dismantling the Triangle powers."

"Isn't it enough to understand it and move on? Why does the power have to be destroyed? Who is being hurt and why must everyone else be protected?" Bob asked. "I mean, I'm not complaining about what happened to me. My wish came true."

"Yes, in your case it did. But, the powers of the Triangle can devastate people's lives."

Unbeknownst to Brooke, Bob had another plan. He was supportive of having Brooke and her colleague solve the mystery, but now that the plan was to destroy the force, he had to act so that would not happen.

"I've instructed my pilot to take us to Las Vegas following our meeting in Memphis. You will be safe from harm, but I want no part in destroying the force."

"Am I being kidnapped? Is that what you are saying? Why not fly directly to Vegas, if that is the case?"

"I want to continue with the meeting in Memphis. Others know you are going there and not showing up would signal a nationwide hunt. We will meet with Mr. Nicklaus and then go to Vegas."

Brooke listened and realized that she was about to become a victim.

Chapter Twenty-Five

While Brooke was high above southern Indiana, Luciano was in the County Building looking over some legal papers for the building of the hospital. Unfortunately, he didn't find any blueprints, or a site plan for the hospital. What he did find was the name of the company that designed the hospital: Lopez Brothers. He asked if this company still existed and was told that it did not. But the company now known as Facilities Engineers bought Lopez Brothers early in the 20th century. Facilities Engineers was located in town and so Luciano drove to their corporate offices and met with the owner, Dick Trap.

"I've got my fingers crossed, that in the archives of your company, might be a site plan or a blueprint, if you will, for the old mental hospital that used to be where the Ghostly Links Country Club is now located. Am I in luck?"

"You might be. When we bought the company from Mr. Lopez, we made sure that past records were maintained. My great grandfather had an eye for history and believed that everything, sooner or later, would be of interest to someone. Guess he knew that you might come knocking on the door. Unfortunately over the years, while we kept the records we have not done so in a professional manner. They are stored in our basement and who knows what shape they might be in. You're welcome to look around."

"Thank you very much. I'll leave everything where I found it and will come back to let you know what I found, should I find something helpful."

"That would be fine. I would like to know."

Luciano was taken to the basement and the door to the storage room was unlocked. It was, as Mr. Trap had said, a musty place with boxes and boxes of materials.

Luciano discovered that all the boxes were labeled, by project, and by year. Not only that, but each box was stacked in the order of the year the project was developed. So, it was just a matter of finding the words "Mental Hospital" or some such identifier before the material Luciano sought would be found. He moved each box, as if rearranging the room, and he couldn't help but think that as is usually the case in searches like this, that the last box in the room would be the one he was looking for.

※

Brooke's feelings for Mr. Rule had changed from a kind benefactor who was supportive of her efforts to solve the case to a man intent on interfering with the goals of the investigation. She felt like a fly that trusted the spider and then by morning found her legs mired in a sticky web.

The plane swooped down west of Memphis and landed. The plane taxied up to the terminal and the four occupants walked out. Mr. Rule's assistant now had the responsibility for seeing that Brooke was always within her sight.

The pilot was released until the flight to Vegas was ready to take off. Brooke, Bob, and Cassandra walked into the headquarters and asked to see Mr. Nicklaus. He was paged by the receptionist and the three were asked to take a seat in the lobby.

Mr. Nicklaus appeared, greeted his guests and led them to a room that contained all the technology one could desire. He invited all to sit around a conference table.

"What can we do for you, Miss Parmore?" Mr. Nicklaus asked.

"As I mentioned over the phone, we have discovered a tunnel in a triangle section of a golf course in the upper Midwest and we've also discovered some interesting properties of the area. I have a videotape which will give you some information. Would you like to see it?"

"Most definitely."

"The first is one in which you will see our robot which we named 'Casper,' by the way, little humor there. Anyway, you will see the interior of the Triangle, a small portion of it, and then the robot will go down a tunnel until it comes to an intersection of tunnels. Then it encounters some force that causes it to, in my words, begin to melt down. That is the end of the first tape. Let's look at it now.

The four watched the tape. This is the first time Bob Rule and Cassandra had ever seen the inside of the tunnel.

The three watched attentively on the very large screen in the NASA conference room. Brooke thoroughly enjoyed the huge picture having only seen the images on a small television monitor. They reacted as expected when they saw the very old man and the change from the teenage girl to an old woman and the gradually sloping tunnel just before the tape stopped.

"So you lost your robot, I take it?" Mr. Nicklaus asked.

"No, my dog Lucky, which is another story, went in and pulled it out. Apparently, the further into the tunnel you go, the older you get or the older the material that makes up the robot gets. Then, when you reverse it, the younger you get and the younger the material gets and you come back to the age you were when you went into the tunnel in the first place."

While Brooke was talking, it dawned on her that Carolyn entered as a teenage girl and not as an older woman with the pastoral golf league. So, that wasn't the first time that Carolyn Spiker had gone into the Triangle. She knew what she was doing. The thought stayed with Brooke as she continued introducing the problem to the others.

"The second tape will show you some ghosts and three ghosts in particular who we think are central to the entire mystery."

The second tape was played and when Dr. Sister, Winnie and Bea came into view, Bob Rule suddenly became frightfully ill and staggered from the room to a bathroom. Mr. Nicklaus followed, concerned for his guest.

"He must have seen something that was very disturbing," Brooke said to Cassandra. "Perhaps you should go to his side. He may need medical assistance or perhaps Mr. Nicklaus will need some information about him."

"Something is very wrong with Mr. Rule," Mr. Nicklaus said quite concerned as he briefly returned from the bathroom. "We're getting medical attention for him."

"May I see you," Mr. Nicklaus said to Cassandra. "We'll need some papers filled out." Brooke rewound the videotape and placed it in its protective box.

Cassandra, concerned for her boss, rose from her chair and went to his side. Brooke took a slip of paper and wrote, "Mr. Nicklaus. I'm very indebted to you for your interest in our project and for reasons, I cannot describe, I must leave. Here is my card; please contact me when things settle. I will explain all that I can. I'm sorry."

Brooke placed the note on Mr. Nicklaus's open leather notebook and picking up her purse, papers, and the two videotapes, she calmly walked to the door and exited. She continued to the front door of the facility.

Brooke showed her pass to the guard and went out to catch a cab. "Memphis Airport, please."

"Yes, ma'am."

The cab pulled up in front of American Airlines. Brooke exited and walked to reservations. She booked a flight home and as luck would have it, a seat was available. The flight left in an hour and soon Brooke was in the air heading home. What a bust, she thought. She was safe and left to ponder what all of that was about. There was no question that Mr. Rule was repulsed by seeing Dr. Sister, Winnie and Bea. He might have had a heart attack or as Cassandra might possibly claim, had his coffee poisoned by Brooke Parmore.

Chapter Twenty-Six

Bob Rule was taken to the hospital for an evaluation. He did have a mild heart attack and was given a series of tests. While doing the evaluation, Dr. Maria Zaharias noted a strange growth on Bob's back and questioned him about it. Bob told her that it was a growth that his doctor had determined to be benign and of no concern at this time. Dr. Zaharias noted the growth and thought it unnecessary to give it additional attention.

From the tests it was determined that Bob did not need immediate surgery. Bob had made it clear that he wanted to return to his own doctor and since he had a corporate jet that would have him home in a couple of hours, he was released with a report to be given to his doctor.

Bob Rule questioned Cassandra concerning Brooke's whereabouts.

"I came to your aid when the NASA gentleman asked to see me. I thought your life was more important than shadowing Miss Parmore. If I erred, I'm sorry."

"That's fine. You did the right thing."

"What happened?"

"My system went berserk when I saw my family."

"Your family?"

"Yes, you must never tell a soul, but that tall man was my father, the older lady was my mother and the other woman was my sister."

"You've never spoken of any family, Mr. Rule. What, if I may ask, would be so shocking to your system?" Cassandra asked.

"I can't talk about it."

"Of course, forgive me for asking such a personal question."

"Let's get back to Chicago."

Brooke arrived home late in the afternoon. She called Larry from the airport to report her safe return. She told him the afternoon had been an adventure to say the least and that she'd give him details later. Then she called Luciano to let him know that she looked forward to relaying what she had experienced. The last place Luciano expected Brooke to be was in Memphis, Tennessee.

"Did you learn anything of importance to our study?" Luciano asked.

"Actually, no. Bob Rule became very ill when Dr. Sister, Winnie and Bea came onto the screen. He gasped, turned pale, got up and managed to get to a bathroom. He was attended to and I have no idea what happened after that. I left the building, took a cab to the airport, and headed home.

"I'll probably have the FBI or CIA knocking on my door or waiting for me when I get home. I mean, I asked for a meeting which was granted the same day. I bring two people with me and one becomes ill and then I up and walk out leaving the NASA folks in a desperate medical situation. I'm sure they thought some international conspiracy was underway."

"I can't believe you got in within a few hours," Luciano said, astonished at what he had heard. "They'd have to do security checks on everyone. I also can't believe they would let the corporate jet land without extensive security checks. That is very strange. Wouldn't you agree, Brooke?"

"Yes, now that you mention it. I just wanted to run something by some folks who may have the technology and/or equipment to get us into the tunnels."

"You haven't heard from the NASA contact since you left?" Luciano asked.

"No, that's what I mean about having the law enforcement folks knocking on my door. Lucky is probably giving them a hard time."

"Well, my day pales in comparison to yours."

"What did you learn?" Brooke asked.

"I learned that I have allergies as a result of breathing horrific air in the basement of the County Building. I did find a box of materials related to the mental health hospital. It was built around 1870. It was a monstrous structure. I found an extensive network of tunnels. The network allows travel between all of the seventeen buildings on the grounds."

"Seventeen buildings?"

"Yes, you have the administration building, the housing units, the horse barn, the hospital, of course, the superintendent's home and a variety of other buildings. All quite full and functioning at one time."

"Must be almost a mile of tunnel?" Brooke asked.

"Yeah, probably. But there's more than a network of tunnels. There is a fairly large room underground as well. One of the tunnels leads to it. I couldn't find the purpose of the room. I don't know if it was for storage or a secure place in case of fire or what. I just don't know because there was no notation identifying the room. The tunnels, by the way, are quite large. A lot of work went into them. I mean, they must be more than six feet tall and at least five feet wide, I suppose to accommodate patients who had to be transported. My guess is, in its day it was a very common corridor for employees and patients. There were provisions for signs directing people to various buildings."

"What did they do about ventilation back then? Did they have vents to the outside or some way to allow for the movement of air?"

"I didn't look for that in the plans. Good question, Brooke."

"Where in comparison to the course is the big room that you mention?"

"As best I can tell, it is almost directly under the clubhouse."

"Really?"

"Well, my guess is that the clubhouse is not directly over it, but a part of the club house would be."

"How far underground does it appear the tunnels are?"

"It looks like they had about ten feet of ground cover. In some spots a bit less as the grounds have some sloping terrain, but they definitely are not close to the surface."

"What are the tunnels made of?"

"According to what I read, they are tile-covered. Now what is under the tile, I can't be certain, but the plans called for tile and some marble, but I'm not sure where the marble was used."

"What are the possibilities of drilling down into the large room?"

"I'd say pretty good. I have no idea what we will find there, Brooke."

"Would we need a large auger, for example?"

"I wouldn't go that far," Luciano replied. "All we really need is a hole. We can then let down a mini-optic device and it will allow us to see what is in there."

"Really? That's possible?" Brooke asked.

"Oh yes, it was used when the terrorists struck New York in 2001. The police would slip it under a hotel room door and be able to see the contents of the room. We can do the same here."

"I have no idea what would come flying up once the hole is created. Maybe we would be releasing a lot of energy in some form? Maybe a deadly gas would come pouring out and infect thousands of people?"

Luciano responded, "I have no idea, but my guess is none of that would happen because the tunnels have outlets. We know one is in the Triangle and one is at the county jail. So, any seepage of gas or pent up energy would seem to dissipate out of those openings."

"That's a good point."

"I think we need to talk to Larry and see what his thoughts are on all of this," Brooke said.

"It might be a good idea. We must have his permission to dig down from under the clubhouse since that couldn't be done without a lot of people gawking and wondering what's going on. I can't think of a more private entrance into that large room than through the basement of the clubhouse."

"What if we release a lot of ghosts?" Brooke asked.

"Well, maybe they'd like a little fresh air, you know?"

"That's humorous. Maybe it isn't a good idea."

"As I said, let's talk to Larry and see what he says."

"I've got to get home," Brooke said. "I'm about to leave the airport and I could be at your hotel by 9:00. I'll call Larry and see if he could join us. If he can, the three of us will meet around 9:00 in the lobby; if he can't, we'll meet first thing in the morning."

"Fine. If you find FBI and CIA folks in your drive and you need a little support, give me a call."

"I will. You're on full alert."

❦

There were no government cars in Brooke's driveway and no indication that anyone had been at her house. Lucky was ecstatic to see Brooke who fed him, rubbed his ears, and took him for a short walk. Before going to the hotel, she checked her mail, and found nothing but junk mail. She checked phone messages and found she had three, but none of them were from Mr. Nicklaus in Memphis. She changed her clothes and got into some slacks and a sweatshirt as it was becoming quite cool. The early morning rain lasted into the afternoon and brought a cold front with it. The air was quite refreshing compared to a muggy Memphis.

Larry was able to meet. At exactly 9:00 the three of them greeted each other and decided to meet in the bar. It was relatively quiet on this week night. The three found a table in the corner, which gave them some privacy. They ordered drinks and began to talk.

Larry was filled in and then Brooke asked, "Larry, what is the chance of your approving the digging of a small hole from your basement into a large room which we believe is under your clubhouse?"

"No way. No way, because of the damage it will cause. No way, because I don't know what will come up from the hole and the members have spent millions to create a clubhouse that is to their liking."

"May we dig a hole on the side of the clubhouse, as long as it is outside?" Brooke asked, continuing the negotiation.

182

"That's much more reasonable, Brooke, but I really don't want to do it."

"What's your fear?" Brooke asked. "I'm not arguing with you; just help me understand what you're thinking."

"It's going to interfere with the landscaping around the clubhouse. That is a minor concern, but again, the members have about had it with this Triangle business and they value the esthetics of their club, so digging will not be appreciated. Again, I don't know what will be released into the air, and if it is a gas, or even a lot of dust spores and stuff, being close to the clubhouse, that toxic stuff could come into the air ducts and could endanger the lives of our members, Finally, ghosts could come pouring out, finally having an escape from their imprisonment."

"Ghosts could come pouring out?" Brooke asked. "You really think that would happen, Larry? I didn't think spirits could be imprisoned."

"Well, you saw them all on the second videotape last night and I think that's just the tip of the iceberg. I don't know if you and Luciano have been able to research the number of patients they had in that hospital while it was in existence. If you did, you'd find that it numbered in the thousands. People die, it's human nature. I think the room could be stacked with ghosts just waiting for the chance to burst forth."

"I agree that you could be right. But, it could also be a command center for Dr. Sister," Luciano replied.

"Yes, it could," Brooke said. "You've got a good point there. He needed a place to go to conduct his experiments. Every doctor and nurse probably was not 100 percent supportive of his interfering with human nature."

"Larry, I want this over as much as you do," Luciano said, honestly. He was ready to get back to New Jersey. "I don't want to keep seeing you so upset with all the attention this beautiful country club is getting. But, I will plead with you, as Father Jim was pleading with us last night to let us get down to that room."

"Tell me what is involved," Larry said, softening a bit to the suggestion.

"We need to drill a hole, probably the size of a baseball," Brooke began. "We would have to drill down and then when we come to the ceiling of the large room we'd have to drill through that. Then we would drop an optic device into the open space and look around. That's all. If something comes up, it comes up, but I don't think it will because I believe there are other ventilations."

"Can the digging be done under the cover of darkness?" Larry asked.

"Most definitely," Luciano replied. "We would be finished in a few hours and your landscaping would look like nobody had even walked in the area."

"OK, let's get it over with," Larry said, finally giving in to the request. "This is getting to the end of my patience, though."

"I have a sense this will be our last request, Larry," Brooke said, thinking the case was close to being history.

"I'll call the professor and tell him of our plans," Larry said. "Hopefully, he will be able to get resources from the university to complete the job tonight."

Professor Divotski was more than willing to help. It would take him awhile to round up the equipment needed for the drilling and the optical scanner. Around midnight the drill was held above a spot which, if Luciano's measurements were correct, would go through the far right side of a room ten to twelve feet underground.

The drill was easily penetrating the earth. Brooke was watching for the drill to hit something solid when her cell phone rang.

"Hmm, at this hour? Hope it isn't the police looking for me."

"It's probably Lucky telling you to get home and get to bed," Larry said, jokingly.

"Hello,"

"Miss Parmore, this is Cassandra Pepper."

"Why are you calling me?" Brooke asked, remembering her role in the planned kidnap.

"I'm sorry to call you at this late hour, very sorry, as I don't like to be disturbed myself, but I thought you would want to know something."

"I'm always hungry for information. What do you have for me?"

"I thought long and hard if I should tell you this, as I was asked by Mr. Rule not to say anything to anyone, so I am violating his trust. But, for the overall good, I want to share information because I believe I can trust you, Miss Parmore."

"What do you have for me, Cassandra?"

"Mr. Rule had a mild heart attack in Memphis. It was triggered when he saw the video of the inside of the Triangle. It happened when he saw the images of the three ghosts. He told me never to tell anyone, but his father is Dr. Sister, his mother is Winnie, and his sister is Bea. I asked him what was so terrible about seeing them that would cause him to react the way he did. He wouldn't tell me that.

"But something was said on the plane going home that is the reason for my call. He told me never to tell anyone, but again, for the good of all, I have chosen to tell you."

"Thank you for your confidence."

"He told me that the power to control the world can be found in a large room within a network of tunnels under the golf course. These tunnels used to be under a mental health complex. I'm sure you know this, but I'm telling you what he told me."

"Power to control the world?" Brooke asked, astonished at what she had just heard. "How could that be?"

"I wondered that, too. He said that the doctor that we saw in the video had perfected a force field and a chip that would grant anyone who entered the field any wish they had, but that at any time all the people ever granted a wish and implanted with the chip could be called back to the Triangle and would have their physical body destroyed."

"Yes, we know this," Brooke said. "Telling me this information confirms our suspicions."

"You asked how the world can be controlled by power in the room."

"Yes, did he tell you that," Brooke asked as the drill hit the ceiling of the underground room.

"He said that the room is completely sealed and has been for decades. This was by design. In the room is a collection of tens of thousands of ghosts and these ghosts are warriors to be used by an alien force who plan to take control of the planet and claim it for the Zolofte Galaxy."

"What power?" Brooke asked, as the drill worked to penetrate the room's ceiling.

"At the moment the room becomes unsealed, the world would be exposed to an energy so great as to be unimaginable. The release of this force would cause thousands to be pulled to the Triangle. They would have no choice but to feel themselves drawn to the Triangle. Once inside, they are under the control of beings from the Zolofte Galaxy.

"Furthermore, the ghosts, once released, will become warriors for beings from the Zolofte Galaxy. These warriors will be used to take over the world and they don't realize this. Becoming a warrior for the Zolofte Galaxy is the payback for having an earthly wish fulfilled."

"Stop! Stop! Stop!" Brooke shouted to the man operating the drill. "God forbid, stop the drill!!!!"

The man doing the drilling apparently didn't hear the warning. He felt the drill go through. As he was pulling the auger out of the hole, Brooke ran to the man, grabbing a shovel on the way, and just as the auger came out of the hole, Brooke slammed the shovel over the hole and stood on it.

"What's going on, Brooke?" Luciano shouted.

"Get this hole filled and don't let any opening appear."

"What's the problem?" Larry asked.

"I can't explain now. Larry, do whatever it takes to contact cement mixing companies and as soon as possible, get a convoy of cement trucks out here, with enough cement to fill a room the size shown in your blueprint."

Still standing on the shovel, Brooke picked up the phone. "Hello, Cassandra? Are you still there?"

"Yes, what happened to you?"

"You just saved the world, Cassandra. You literally just saved the world."

"There is a way to harness the energy, Brooke," Cassandra said holding the solution to the crisis.

"What is that?" Brooke said desperate for a solution.

"Fire. Mr. Rule told me that fire consumes the force and renders it useless."

"Will there be a gigantic explosion?" Brooke asked.

"He didn't say, but I think if there would be, he would have said so."

"Stay on the line, Cassandra. Don't hang up."

"Luciano, go to Larry and tell him to scrap the cement truck caravan. Tell him to come here quickly."

Within a few seconds, Larry came running to Brooke. "What do you need?"

"We've got to build a bonfire over this hole. I know your members don't want this to happen, but for the sake of the world, it has to happen, Larry. I'll explain it all later, but we need a fire, now!"

Larry went off to the trash barrels and got plenty of cardboard boxes and began to carry wood from the woodpile used for winter cross-country ski parties. Within minutes cardboard paper and wood were positioned over the hole.

Brooke noticed that people were marching to the Triangle. The line went on and on and the orderly progression snaked its way to the Triangle from as far away as she could see. She thought she had to be dreaming. People of all ages, wearing clothes from the present moment to decades ago, rich and poor, were making their way to the Triangle.

Brooke glanced toward the Triangle and under a clear sky and moonlit night she saw thousands of people standing around the Triangle. There was no noise, just the presence of hundreds of people, a fifteen-to twenty-foot-deep collection of souls, surrounding the perimeter of the Triangle, and more were coming from as far as she could see.

The auger was moved close to Brooke who remained standing on the shovel where the hole had been dug. Brooke explained that as soon as she took the shovel away from the hole, the auger must immediately go into the ground and forced all the way through to the room. Then he was to slowly bring it up. Before doing so the fire was to be lit so that when he removed the auger any escaping vapor would be consumed in flames. The fire would be fed throughout the night.

After instructions were given, Brooke got back on the phone, "Cassandra, are you still there?"

"Yes, Brooke. I can't imagine what is going on."

"I'll share it all with you in time, but your call literally saved planet Earth and this will become clear to you when we can meet and I can explain it all in detail."

"OK, I hope this has helped."

"Actually you and Bob Rule saved our planet, for if he had not told you and you had not chosen to disclose it, by now, the energy, the force, would have begun a cloud that would devastate this city, county, state and who knows if it would ever end."

"Oh, my God, really?" Cassandra said, realizing the part she played in helping avert a disaster of humongous proportions.

"That's right. We came so close to self-destructing. God bless you, Cassandra."

"Well, you know I wasn't going to tell you this either, but something really scary happened before I called. It shook me to the core."

"What was that?"

"I was visited by a ghost."

"Really?" Brooke said.

"Yes, this ghost slowly turned into a person. I was in a state of shock. Anyway, the ghost became a man and this man told me to call you, even giving me your number, and he told me what to tell you."

"Really?"

"Yes."

"You did the right thing, by the way. What was his name, or can you describe him?"

"I don't know his name, but I think he was a religious man. He had on one of those clerical collars that Catholic priests wear. He left quickly saying that he was being called home."

Chapter Twenty-Seven
Friday, September 2, 2005

The fire burned throughout the night. The police were called and were able to keep curious people at a distance. Everyone standing around the Triangle remained whole. Nobody went into the Triangle nor did anyone disintegrate. In fact, in the same fashion as they arrived, they left.

The sun rose. Larry, Brooke and Luciano were exhausted. They had been up since yesterday morning. They stood and hugged one another. They knew that what had happened in the last twenty-four hours was powerful with catastrophic consequences.

The golf course was closed. A barricade was constructed across the driveway and all members were asked to call a number if they wished information. Larry had recorded a brief explanation of what had happened.

Professor Divotski, Tom and Cheri arrived late the next morning. Brooke had called and asked them to arrive around 10:00 or so with the robot. Brooke was able to go home for a short nap, to take care of Lucky, and then she returned to the golf course.

A very tired trio of Larry, Luciano and Brooke greeted the professor and students. The plan was discussed and it was for Casper to go into the Triangle and to enter the tunnel to see if any change may have occurred due to the opening of the large room and the four plus hours of screaming and wailing sounds as the gas, if that is what it was, came up from the command center.

The purpose of Casper's work was to look for ghosts and to determine if the robot would begin to melt again as it went through the tunnel.

With preparations in place, the device was activated and Casper was guided into the Triangle. The camera was turned on and nothing out of the ordinary was seen. It looked like a normal woods on a golf course, but then again, so did the previous transmission when Casper went in during daylight. The professor guided the robot to the entrance of the tunnel and allowed it to move along taking pictures. This time, no ghosts were visible and the robot moved along normally without slowing down.

The robot toured for well over an hour until its energy capacity was beginning to signal that little power was left. The robot was able to enter the command room and those looking at the monitor saw a typical laboratory with lots of cabinets and closets.

A second warning flashed and the professor said, "I must bring him out or he'll be stuck in there."

"No, problem, bring him out. We've seen all we need to see," Brooke said.

"The tunnels seemed to be clear. Maybe the force has all been sucked out and the underground system is clean." Luciano said.

"I don't know where we will find someone willing to risk going in to see if in fact, it is anything more than old tunnels under this world famous course," Brooke said.

Just then, to the surprise of everyone, Father Jim McDuffy walked up and joined the group.

"Father Jim! So good to see you!" Brooke exclaimed.

"Thank you. I see your free choice caused you not to take my advice."

"I knew you would be disappointed, but we all agreed to keep on investigating. We needed to solve this."

"Well, you do have free will and your decisions are yours to make."

"Thank you for all you've done, Father."

"Whoa, let's not give me too much credit here. I simply told Miss Pepper to give you a call. Again, your free choice caused you to act in a way that kept the force enclosed. I didn't do that, you did."

"But if it hadn't been for your intervening, it would have been disastrous."

"I guess you're right. Brooke, I'm willing to go into the Triangle and prove that what was once feared is no longer a concern for anyone."

"Oh, no, Father, you've already done enough to save the planet."

"It will not be a problem for me. I've been in many times and my wishes have all come true. I'll miss that, but let me walk in and go through all the tunnels and the command room so that you can tell the world that the Triangle at Ghostly Links is safe."

"Thank you, Father," Brooke said and gave him a hug.

All watched as Father Jim walked down to the Triangle and walked in. He stooped down to pick up a few coins. The collection plate could use a few coins he thought, and he also picked up a half dozen golf balls. He didn't get as many golf balls as he had hoped for last Christmas and these would come in handy.

Father Jim entered the cave-like opening. As he walked along with a flashlight, he looked into all tunnel passages. He went into the command room and noted the hole in the ceiling. There was nothing strange about the room. He opened a cabinet and found hundreds of chips. It also was obvious that the laboratory had been used until the minute the fire began. He felt certain that Dr. Sister had been there activating the chips, calling everyone to the Triangle for their physical death.

As Father Jim was about to leave, he noticed a file that was labeled, "The Beginning." He opened it and read:

It is in the middle of the night and the predawn hours of September 3, 1925. I've just had a strange experience. What is recorded here is my memory of what was said. In some cases, I am paraphrasing as my memory of exact words is lacking. I am still stunned and feeling a bit strange. I wanted to capture the experience. Our dialogue follows.

Alien: I have come to seek your support for an eighty-year-project that will require your superior intelligence. You earthly beings need to be motivated and so I have come to propose eternal life if you will do as I say.

Sam: I will only be motivated to seek eternal life if I know what you would have me do for such a reward.

Alien: That is fair. I will explain. I come from the Zolofte Galaxy. I have been sent by my supreme leader who has determined that earth is a planet that we would like to inhabit. But to do this, we must be able to overcome any resistance. We believe that frequent trips to earth will result in many attacks and we are not wishing to fight. We have risen to a higher standard of conduct. Therefore, it is my mission to ask you to recruit for us. If you are willing to cooperate, you will be given all the tools you need to assist us.

Sam: Tools?

Alien: You will be able to grant a wish to all who you are able to entice to the field of energy currently being deposited under this craft. Once a human being enters this triangular field, their wish will be granted and they will instantly live on two planes, a physical plane and a spiritual plane. A chip will be implanted in their bodies which will have a dual purpose. The chip will assure their wish to come true, but more importantly for us, in the Zolofte Galaxy; they will be called back to this site on September 3, 2005 to participate in our gaining control of planet Earth.

Sam: How will the chips be implanted?

Alien: Time will be suspended for the earthling. He will think a second to a few minutes has passed when in fact it has been several cosmic days so that the chip can be implanted and healed.

Sam: Any wish is granted?

Alien: Yes, any wish that is in the human's subconscious. The human need not even express a wish. Every human who enters the space, with even so little as a hand or foot into the triangular force field, will have the wish granted and a chip implanted.

Sam: I'm still not certain of my role.

Alien: You will maintain records, the human's name, wish, and date of chip implant. This is important. When any human dies a physical death, the ghost of that human instantly returns to this triangular home. The ghosts take up no room per sé. They will report in and they will be kept in your underground laboratory. They may be free to roam about the area, but have no fear; they are programmed to return to your laboratory.

Sam: So, am I like a recruiter? For eternal life, I need to get thousands of people to come to the Triangle so that they become unsuspecting warriors for the takeover of planet Earth by the Zolofte Galaxy. Correct?

Alien: Yes, and, we are establishing this energized force field here on the hospital grounds so that you will always have a steady supply of humans. Should this land be used for something else, you will have to use your intelligence to continue to seek warriors.

Sam: If the word gets out that a wish will come true if a person comes into this triangular piece of land, the place will be frequented by thousands if not millions of people.

Alien: Precisely. For their wish being granted on the physical plane, they become our warriors when we return on September 3, 2005.

Sam: Is there anything than can destroy this collection of ghosts?

Alien: Yes, fire.

Sam: Back to my eternal life. I will live forever on the earth?

Alien: You will live forever on the physical plane and on the spiritual plane unless...

Sam: I thought there would be a catch.

Alien: Unless humans at any point discover our

collection of ghosts and destroy our warriors. If this happens, you will die, because if you agree to be our ally, you will be implanted with a chip so that you can have eternal life, but also so we can destroy you should our plan fail.

Sam: I will accept your proposal and will recruit people for the Zolofte Galaxy to take over the world in 2005 on September 3. Can I share any of this with another?

Alien: Yes, you have free will as do humans, but you always know that if sharing what you know causes you to fail, you will die.

Sam: One more question. Am I correct that I can live on the physical and spirit planes at the same time?

Alien: Yes, and so will all that you recruit. They will have a choice, to live on a physical plane, a spirit plane, or both at the same time.

Sam: And they will never know that they are recruited warriors for the Zolofte Galaxy?

Alien: Correct. You must always be at this site, in physical or spirit form. While one form is here, your other form can be elsewhere. Did I understand you to say, you are willing to assist us?

Sam: Yes. Will I always be in contact with you?

Alien: No, this is your only contact. Everything should be clear when you leave this craft.

Sam: I understand. I accept the consequences of a failed effort. There is no quota, am I correct?

Alien: We expect one million warriors.

Sam: Am I it or are you singling out others at other spots around the world.

Alien: You are it. Before we go, I must tell you that you will hear of flying saucers being seen and aliens coming to earth. This will not be true as far as the Zolofte galaxy is concerned. We will arrive on September 3, 2005 to direct the actions of our one million warriors as we secure earth for our galaxy.

Father Jim opened a cabinet and took some files to give to Brooke. The files were extensive lists of people's names, the wish that was granted and the date the warrior had been given a wish and a chip.

As he was about to leave he saw a note on top of a desk. He picked it up and read, "Should any human find this note, it will mean that the seal of the laboratory has been broken. The original intent of the Triangle was to bring joy to others by granting them their wishes, but if my laboratory is damaged and my ghostly geniuses, the warriors of the Zolofte Galaxy, are destroyed, I will have failed to secure the million warriors needed by the aliens. I have no choice but to seek out the people responsible for my demise and destroy them. I have discovered the secret to granting wishes perfected by the geniuses from the Zolofte Galaxy." It was signed, "Dr. S. Sister."

Father Jim made a quick decision not to share this note with Brooke or Luciano, because he was certain that Dr. Sister's spirit form had perished in the fire. Besides, it would serve no purpose. He had asked the two to refrain from investigating the Triangle and they had chosen not to. Giving them Dr. Sister's note would only serve to challenge Brooke and Luciano even further and that could lead to chaos that could further threaten the world as they knew it. He put the note in his pocket and would destroy it later.

Father Jim walked through the tunnels and out of the Triangle. He headed up to the clubhouse.

"I am sure you will want to thoroughly study the laboratory and the thousands of files therein. It is safe to go in. There are no powers, no ghosts. I picked up a few coins and six golf balls, Larry. Could this be my reward for the journey?"

"Yes, Father. If more money is in the Triangle, it will all go to charity."

"The floor of the Triangle has money all over the place and while I only picked up six good golf balls, they're all over in there too. Here are some files that were in a filing cabinet. I suggest you read the top file. It will explain everything."

Brooke took the musty files and opened one of them. There before her eyes was the dialogue that began this mystery, 80 years ago tomorrow. She also glanced at the names of hundreds who had entered the Triangle during the past 80 years and it also included the names of everyone who had visited the Triangle since the golf course opened on July 4, 1999.

While Brooke was counting the names and reading a few of the wishes that had been granted, one by one some people began coming to the golf course. Each was permitted past the barricade to see Brooke Parmore. Lucy Putterbee introduced herself and said that her piano playing ability was gone. Rick said he no longer had mastery over pitching a baseball. Cliff said he had his damaged heart back. The Special Olympic golfer suddenly lost a great deal of intelligence. Bea came into the room and gave Brooke a hug, tears forming in her eyes. Bob Rule appeared unable to read and was a common man as far as wealth goes.

The people continued to stop in, and while they felt they were normal once again, they did enjoy having had their wishes fulfilled. But, they were equally thrilled that the threat to be called home to death at any second had been destroyed.

By the end of the day, the people had stopped coming and for the first time in weeks, all seemed uncharacteristically calm and normal.

Luciano gathered up his things and made plans to return to New Jersey. He would appear on the NBC *Today* Show in the morning. The country was curious about this threat to their existence.

Brooke saw Larry alone in the pro shop. She approached him and took a deep breath. "Thank you very much. Your support was marvelous and we couldn't have solved it without you. I will always be indebted to you, honey. I hope you know that."

"Yes, dear, I know. But, it was you who figured it all out. You saved the planet because had you not covered that drilled hole down into the laboratory the force would have been out." Brooke moved close to give him a kiss and a hug. They were both relieved that the ordeal was finally over. All thoughts could now be focused on their wedding.

Ghostly **LINKS**

Luciano had a few hours before his flight and there was sufficient light to allow him to play nine holes. He took advantage of the opportunity. He was alone, playing the 157-yard, par-3, 5th hole. The ball went skyward in perfect alignment with the flagstick. The ball landed on the fringe of the green, bounced twice and rolled right up to the cup and fell in. Luciano ran all the way to the green to see the little white ball resting in the bottom of the cup. He'd done it, a hole in one. It would not be official as it wasn't witnessed, but the dream had come true.

Luciano looked around for evidence of spirits and found none. It appeared that the perfect shot could be attributed to his skill and not to the presence of helpful ghosts. Luciano stood on the green, kissed the ball, and smiled a wide and happy grin. *Oh happy day!* Luciano thought.

Chapter Twenty-Eight
Saturday, September 3, 2005

When Brooke awoke the next morning she turned on the TV and enjoyed the NBC interview of Luciano. During a light breakfast she became curious about a few people. She called the number she had for Winnie. As she expected, the phone was not answered. She called the nursing home in Sudbury to ask if Doctor Sister had returned. She was told, no.

That was it, she thought, the door would be closed on a very interesting and difficult case that almost got away. Suddenly, Brooke's cell phone rang.

"Hello."

"Miss Parmore, This is Winnie Palmer. I'm sorry I didn't answer when you called. We have caller ID. I wanted to see who was calling and thought I saw another name. I am home. Dr. Sister is here, too. Would you like to come over for some tea?"

Epilogue

Cliff and Jane were playing golf again. Cliff was already gaining back a lot of weight and his heart made getting around difficult. But, and perhaps most importantly, he took another lesson from Larry Ball and his shots were going fairly straight down the fairway.

The religious golf league was back to normal with the community religious leaders enjoying each other's company and relaxing a bit on the links.

Lucy Putterbee continued to provide piano lessons for Rick as she now realized the joy of playing the instrument.

Rick Putterbee's pitching woes returned. He lost his position in the starting rotation of his high school baseball team. His arm became very sore and he was dropped from the team.

Reverend Hogan was once again in the pulpit extolling the virtues of living a life free of sin.

Reverend Spiker was also back in the pulpit at the Episcopal Church. She told everyone she had a dream of being a caddy for a famous woman on the LPGA tour. She laughed as she told of the pro often taking her advice. Carolyn felt that she had a part to play in the tournaments that the pro won during the 2005 season. Pay attention to your dreams, Reverend Spiker told all worshippers.

John was back playing on the Special Olympics golf team.

Bob Rule's company went bankrupt in the economic downturn. He returned to a job in sales.

Eddie Hazard's son Eric called Larry and said that his father seemed to be feeling the effects of arthritis lately. He was doing well and actually enjoying slowing down a bit.

Larry reported that he had received a phone call and the message was left on his answering machine. He hit the play button and heard, "There will be no foundation at Ghostly Links. My skills have mysteriously disintegrated and I can't seem to recover the touch for top competition. There will be no Master's victory in 2006. Thanks for the ride of a lifetime." The caller did not identify himself. Larry erased the tape.

Larry also reported that John Score told him a strange story about his son Lloyd. Apparently, a golf ball that he had found in the Triangle, a Titleist Two, reappeared on top of his dresser in his bedroom. It reappeared as mysteriously as it had left. John said that his son thought it was possessed, so he took it to the Triangle and threw it back in.

The Country Club sponsored a contest to predict the number of golf balls now sitting on the floor of the Triangle. Susie King, a local bowling whiz, won the contest missing by only ten. The correct number of balls in the Triangle was 21,632 (not counting the six that Father Jim took on his way out from inspecting the tunnels for Brooke).

Money was collected from the Triangle. The Boy Scout Troop who did the collecting counted a total of $19,658.75. All of the money would go to local charities, as Larry had promised.

Jessica Pond, the newspaper reporter, won the Pulitzer Prize for excellence in local news reporting with a week-long series of articles following the fire that consumed the spirits of the Triangle.

Sam Player called to say that his wife wanted to see if they could get back together.

Rick Clubb told his superintendent that all of his traps remain smooth and sand castles are a thing of the past.

Bishop Walker could rest more easily in the absence of spirits in his life, except for THE SPIRIT which was always present.

There was a bulletin on the radio saying that the vaccine for polio has been determined after all of these years to be ineffective.

Researchers are taking steps to try and discover the problem and to begin an aggressive effort to develop an effective vaccine.

Professor Divotski, Tom and Cheri were recognized by the department chair and the university president for wonderful work. Research papers were presented at international symposiums and much acclaim came to the University because of the development of Casper the Robot.

Sheriff Woodrough called Brooke and Luciano and thanked them for all they had done to give him the first stress less day of his career.

Father Jim asked to be released from his vows. The Bishop granted his request. He married Sister Mulligan who had also sought permission to be released from her vows. Jim McDuffy became a comedian appearing at Comedy Clubs all over the Midwest. He also became a lecturer telling audiences of his experiences with the Triangle as well as his beliefs. A few believed him, but most thought him to be an opportunist with an overactive imagination.

Cassandra Pepper became a friend of Brooke's and over time became Brooke's research assistant as some very challenging international cases were to be in Brooke's future.

The note that Luke and Cynthia Eagleton's dog brought up from the Triangle said "To date, $9,546.00 has been thrown into this Triangle. It's yours if you come on in to get it." Mrs. Eagleton never understood why Luke didn't go into the Triangle.

Brooke did go to Winnie's home. Her curiosity was too strong. After her visit she went directly to Ghostly Links. She walked into the pro shop, greeted Larry and gave him a hug. As he held her close, he felt a raised bump on her back. He made a mental note to mention it and suggest she have a doctor look at it. He had not felt it before and was concerned.

Luciano DiNatale, once back home in New Jersey, tried to call Brooke. He had seen something that disturbed him. All he heard was a recorded message, "You have reached a non-working number. Please recheck your number and call again, or dial '0' to talk to an operator."

The End

Meridian Sun Golf Club

While there is absolutely no plan to associate real people with the characters in this story, the course in my mind during my writing of this book was my home course, The Meridian Sun Golf Club in Haslett, Michigan. It was on this course that the Triangle called the 'Bermuda Triangle of the Links' was found. The Meridian Sun "Triangle" borders the 12th, 13th, and 4th holes.

The chip to the green before Jane discovered that Cliff had no heart was from the bottom of the incline leading up to the 4th green. Finally, many ideas for this book came while playing rounds at the Meridian Sun Golf Club. I guess I could truly say that I was going to work when I went to Meridian Sun to play.

As my disclaimer notes, this story is strictly a figment of my imagination. There is nothing strange about Meridian Sun, the triangle of land between the 12th, 13th, and 4th holes! But, I wouldn't be surprised if a few rumors are begun by golfers who read this book and then play at Meridian Sun. As one of my characters said, all you need to do is plant something in the imagination for it to express itself.

Thank you for reading my story.

Hit 'em straight and long!

Buttonwood Press Order Form

To order additional copies of *Ghostly Links*, or other books by Richard L. Baldwin, visit the website of Buttonwood Press at www.buttonwoodpress.com for information or fill out the order form here. Thank you.

Name_____

Address _____

City/State/Zip _____

Book Title	Qty	Price
Ghostly Links ($16.95 – Hardcover)		
The Marina Murders ($12.95 – Softcover)		
Buried Secrets of Bois Blanc: Murder in the Straits of Mackinac ($12.95 – Softcover)		
A Lesson Plan for Murder ($12.95 – Softcover)		
The Principal Cause of Death ($12.95 – Softcover)		
Administration Can Be Murder ($12.95 – Softcover)		
TOTAL		

Rich Baldwin will personally autograph a copy of any of his books for you. It's also a great gift for that mystery lover you know!

Autograph Request To:

_____

_____

_____

Mail Order Form with a Check payable to:

Buttonwood Press   Fax: 517-339-5908
PO Box 716   Email: RLBald@aol.com
Haslett, MI 48840   Website: www.buttonwoodpress.com

Questions? Call the Buttonwood Press office at (517) 339-9871. Thank you!